Alt-Ctrl

Rebecca Freeman

Alt-Ctrl
Rebecca Freeman

Thea Press
P.O. Box 24905
Tempe, AZ 85285
USA
www.theapress.com

Cover art by Atomic-75.

For more information about Rebecca Freeman, see http://rebeccafreeman.com.au

First printing, September 2019

ISBN-13: 978-1733506410 (Paperback)
ISBN-10: 1733506410 (Paperback)

For My People –

you know who you are.

Acknowledgements

Hello there! Wow! Thanks so much for reading Alt-Ctrl, or at least picking it up and reading the acknowledgements. As with most stories, this one has taken a long time to complete. Writing can be lonely, and sharing it can be scary, and it's important to have friends you can count on to keep you sane on the journey.

I would firstly like to acknowledge the Minang people, the traditional owners of the country on which Alt-Ctrl was written. It's such a beautiful part of the world and I feel so fortunate to be able to live and work here.

This story began as a NaNoWriMo novel, but that novel and this novella have been through many edits, rewrites, and changes since I started it eight years ago. During this time, I've had so much support. Thanks must therefore go to friends who've read the draft(s) and who've given me valuable, targeted, helpful feedback: Alex Isle, Jeremiah Murphy, Lila Schow, Jodie How, Rachel Watts. Thanks also to all my fellow word-nerds from Writing Group and Scifanthor, who've cheered me on and listened to my readings and not fallen asleep. And obviously to my 5am writers group! What a fantastic bunch, even (especially?) early in the mornings!

I'd like to give a special shout out to Dominica Malcolm of Solarwyrm Press for publishing my short story, 'And then it Rained' in her anthology Amok, which gave me the idea for Alt-Ctrl, and which also helped me to realise that it was a novella I could write.

Of course, my utmost gratitude goes to my publisher, Kate Allen, who saw potential in this story and agreed to send it out into the world.

Thank you to my family who've always been interested in and encouraged my writing – my parents and my siblings – and to Adam, my Handsome Sidekick who has metaphorically kicked me in the butt several times when I wanted to give up but whose belief in me has been resolute and unfailing. I absolutely could not have completed this without you.

And lastly to my children, who are not at all patient when I say I need to write (they're children, after all), but who seem to understand that it's important anyway, and who have delighted in being able to draw pictures on the backs of my copy edits: thank you, and I hope you'll read this story one day and be only mildly disappointed.

Prologue

2039. April.

"It's Eva," said the voice through the speaker.

The Prime Minister jumped at the intrusion, then took a careful, deep breath. She forced a smile into her voice, and turned to the screen.

"Eva! A pleasant surprise."

"Stop lying. It's neither pleasant nor a surprise. You must have been expecting my call. Your payment is late."

"We... we contacted your collections department. They said that they would work with us and get back to us with some kind of payment plan."

"And here it is," replied Eva. "I am getting back to you, personally, to confirm that outstanding payments need to be made to PlanetRescue within 24 hours, or I will begin to shut our Cities down."

The Prime Minister paled.

"You can't be serious! Eva, we just don't have the resources! Why would we keep it from your company if we did?"

She was stumbling over her words, grasping at excuses. Anything to get Eva to change her mind. She rubbed her right temple, trying to smooth out the headache which had been worrying her for the past two days.

"I'll take mercy on you," said Eva.

She sat back, her small frame seeming even smaller against the black leather back of the office chair. Behind her, the Prime Minister could see the outline of Western City and its protective dome through the huge tinted windows. It was unlike Eva to be merciful, but if she were feeling generous, the Prime Minister knew better than to question it.

"Thank you, Eva. I'm sure – "

"I will begin with our smallest Cities first."

The Prime Minister gasped.

"You know how to get in touch," Eva said, calmly. "PlanetRescue expects to hear from you soon."

Chapter 1

2057. March.

Wake up.

Finn turned in her sleep.

Finn. Open your eyes.

Finn woke, but kept her eyes closed. Jhara was contacting her inWorld, and all it required was a shift in her consciousness to connect, and let Jhara know she was awake.

It's early, Finn said. *I'm not due at work for three hours. I hope you've got a good reason for this.*

Stop your grumbling, Jhara replied, the amusement evident. *Anyway, I don't think you'll be needing to go into work.*

Finn opened her eyes and sat up on her sleeping mat, her sudden movement switching on the lights in the room.

What?

It's time, Jhara said. *Meet me and Braithe at my room in five minutes.*

Finn broke the connection so she could better

concentrate. She got up from her mat on the floor, rolled it up, and stowed it in the wardrobe in the corner. Out of habit, she pulled off her dark grey sleeping suit, folded it loosely and put it away. She then grabbed fresh dayclothes from the wardrobe: dark grey leggings and a long-sleeved shirt, all made from the same stretchy hemp fabric. As an afterthought, she took a jacket as well – if Jhara was right, she might need it.

Finn rubbed her stubbled head, and smoothed her hands over her face. Now that she was up, the fatigue from being woken so suddenly was starting to fade, and the anticipation began to tighten in her belly. It was time to set the shutdown in motion, something she had been practising for weeks. She was the best and most efficient worker in her position at WorldSec, the branch dealing with security in the City and which maintained the World, ensuring that Cityzens were only able to access company-approved information. She felt embarrassed at how long it had taken her to question why access to information inWorld, the database accessible by all Cityzens via the port installed in their skulls as infants, should be limited. But at least she had questioned it, with the guidance of Braithe, Jhara's parent, and it had led to this point: the day it was all going to change.

She switched in her mind again, accessing the World, revelling in the familiarity of colours and images which all Cityzens saw when they connected to the virtual environment. Everything was there – entertainment, music, art, and theatre from every culture, stretching back millennia. History, politics, science, mathematics… or at least, that which was approved by PlanetRescue. As one of the few with the highest security clearances, Finn knew that what most Cityzens were able to experience was a tiny fraction of what the World held. Even her own access was limited to ensuring breaches didn't occur. It had taken a long time to work out a way around the limits of WorldSec so that she could learn the history that PlanetRescue didn't want its Cityzens to know.

But right now, Finn didn't need information. She needed to work. She slipped into the Ether, the mechanics behind the World, which only she and some others from WorldSec ever got to see. It was here that Finn began to move through the areas controlling security cameras, gently switching the code in each so that the image seen by WorldSec monitors would be a loop carefully recorded by Finn over the past weeks. The work had been painstaking, and now she was in the final stage. She needed to take her time, not to slip up and alert WorldSec by moving too quickly.

Once done, she was tired, but the excitement spurred her on. Now they were undetectable – at least by the security cameras. They still had to avoid the automated security cars which patrolled all night, ostensibly for the protection of all Cityzens to guard against those from the Badlands, who were reported to have broken in previously, stealing food and causing random damage. Finn remembered her fear from when she was young, the stories everyone whispered about the radiation and how it had turned the Badlanders into monsters, barely human, surviving on roots or insects, or perhaps even each other.

She sighed. Most of the Cityzens still believed this, terrified that their lives under the safety of the City's protective skydome could be destroyed and the hordes of Badlanders would pour in, destroying everything. It was Jhara and Braithe who had explained to Finn that it was all a lie. Far too young to understand at the time, Finn now realised that they had saved her life. Because she had been slow to learn to talk as an infant, she had been designated

Maintenance, and was scheduled to be sent to the Central City. But Braithe knew what this meant, and she took Finn away from the group schooling lessons, for hours at a time, talking and singing to her, until Finn gradually began to be able to talk and sing back, and then rapidly she surpassed her peers in vocabulary and all other academic areas. She still found interaction and small talk uncomfortable, an unnecessary annoyance, but for all its faults, PlanetRescue had found the perfect job for her, and she had exceeded all milestones in her position at WorldSec, where she worked with code and had little to do with people.

Finn.

Jhara sounded impatient.

I'm coming, Finn replied.

She closed the cupboard door and quickly washed her face with the hemp cloth from the drawer in the wall. She put it back in the laundry chute; it would be collected later by Maintenance. Standing near the door, she took a moment to look at herself in the mirror. Short brown hair and green eyes, skin pale from recent sleep. She didn't look as though she were about to take part in a revolution.

Jhara and Braithe were waiting just outside the open

door to Jhara's room, the soft light from inside casting shadows across their faces, so she couldn't see their expressions, even though she knew they'd be a mirror of each other. Jhara was like Braithe's clone: same willowy bodies, same stark black hair pulled back from their faces, same freckled complexion, same deep brown eyes, always ready to smile. Finn was out of breath, having run along corridors and slipped quickly up stairwells. Since the autodrivers took everyone everywhere, Cityzens didn't need to walk far at all – Finn's heart and lungs were protesting at the unusual physical activity.

Jhara laughed.

"All those times you made fun of me walking to work," she said. "Who's laughing now?"

Finn shot her a glance and tried to slow her breathing. Braithe smiled and put a reassuring hand on Finn's shoulder.

"Ignore my rude child," she said. "You've taken care of security?"

Finn nodded, her heart finally slowing.

"All done," she said. "Of course we still need to look for automated security detail. If I'd had more time…"

"You did brilliantly," Braithe reassured her. "And you and

Jhara are quick enough on your feet to avoid them."

Jhara snorted, and Finn gave her a shove.

"Let's just see who does best in the Badlands," Finn said, smugly. "I've been training."

"Wow, you have?" Jhara asked, genuinely surprised.

"Are you kidding?" Finn laughed. "Of course not."

Their giggles were due to nerves more than anything, but it broke the tension. Braithe looked at them both, lips pressed together in mock disapproval.

"This is not going to be easy, for either of you," she said, gently, but here was a serious edge to her voice. "We don't know how long we have until PlanetRescue realises there is something wrong. And we can only hope that Serena and the others are ready. And it is a walk. A long one."

She turned to Finn.

"How long will the loop last?"

"Until they disable it," Finn shrugged, "so as long as it takes for them to notice. It could be as early as a few minutes from now, to late this evening. Or tomorrow. My not going into work later might raise alarms, but I have scheduled an alert to my supervisor..."

Braithe sighed.

"Getting a simple answer from you is certainly a challenge," she said, laughing in spite of her frustration. "Let's just assume we're almost out of time –"

"Well, that's unlikely, too," interrupted Finn.

"Let's *assume*," said Braithe with restraint, "and you need to leave now. You've disabled trackers?"

Finn nodded.

"It was easy. It will seem as if we're still here."

"Good." Braithe seemed content. "I will stay here as planned, and wake up the Underground. I've packed some food for you…"

She reached down and picked up two small backpacks, the kind that PlanetRescue gave to security employees – nicknamed Rescuers – for their rounds. Finn wondered where Braithe had managed to get hold of them. Braithe opened one pack to show them the contents: some containers of regular rations as well as a crinkly silver sheet which she explained would keep them warm at night.

"You'll need to walk as fast as you can, and rest only seldom," she told them.

"We know this," said Jhara, "it's not like we haven't talked about it, over and over."

"Cut your impatience," said Braithe, sharply, and Jhara looked contrite.

It was unlike Braithe to be so angry. She closed her eyes and took a breath.

"I'm sorry. I'm worried. I just want you to be safe, and I need you to get to Seven Rivers. If only I could go myself."

"You know we can do this," Jhara said, putting her hand on her parent's forearm.

"I know," Braithe smiled. "I wouldn't send you if I didn't."

She gathered Jhara in her arms and kissed her on both cheeks. Knowing Finn disliked such close affection, Braithe simply squeezed her shoulder and both young women slipped their arms through the backpack straps.

"Go well," Braithe said, her voice breaking, and slipped back into her room, quickly shutting the door behind her.

Jhara and Finn looked at each other. Jhara shrugged, and with a final glance up and down the corridor, they began to jog towards the end stairwell. Finn's legs felt shaky, both from the exercise and the adrenalin. At the bottom of the stairs, they paused and looked out into the darkness. In the light of the regularly placed streetlamps she could see the corners of each accommodation block, which were different heights and shapes, all sourced from various buildings from before the Collapse. But the light the lamps gave off was poor, to save on power. Their main purpose was to highlight the edge of buildings. This worked in Finn and Jhara's favour; while they had to run in the dark, it also meant that they would be less visible. And since all Cityzens would still be sleeping, no security detail would expect them to be out. They crept forward and slipped out the door and round the side of the block, keeping close to the dark walls.

The City was quiet and warm. Of course, the climate was controlled by the skydome above, which was another innovation by PlanetRescue to protect the Cityzens from the radiation in the Badlands, but also to block out the searing sun, and shelter them from rain and dust storms. Finn looked up and strained to see the dark sky beyond the silvery shimmer of the dome.

Finn thought of the planning she had done with Braithe over the previous months.

"Remember," she had said to them more than once, "people have short memories, when life is going well. We want to forget the hard times. We want the easy life. You might look back on all this and curse all the Cityzens for the power we gave PlanetRescue, but in truth, you cannot judge them, and neither should we. Above everything, people just want to survive."

"Come on!" Jhara whispered harshly interrupting her memory. "You can look at the sky later, when there is actual sky to look at."

Finn glanced behind her to check again if they were being followed. Nothing. She jogged after Jhara and caught up, slowing to a fast walk next to her.

"One more block to go," said Jhara in a low voice. She looked both ways and then darted across the deserted street to the edge of the building on the opposite side.

She motioned for Finn to follow but something wasn't right. Finn shook her head, pressing her body against the wall. Peering carefully around the corner, she looked down the street, straining to hear again the noise.

"What is it?" whispered Jhara urgently.

Finn held up her hand, and listened.

Three blocks away to her right, an automated security detail turned the corner. Finn could see the dull lighting from the block's lamp reflecting off its side. The automated vehicles travelled slowly and almost noiselessly, their headlights like closed eyes. Finn knew that the moment they detected any movement, the headlights would snap on, an alarm would sound in the WorldSec headquarters, and three Rescuers would be dispatched. If that happened, they'd have to abandon their attempt – Rescuers were thorough and would almost certainly find them if they were out in the open.

Finn looked across at Jhara. She had seen it, too, and looked panicked. Finn drew her head back slowly behind the corner and held up a hand to Jhara.

Wait there.

Finn looked behind her, along the street where they'd just walked. There was nothing. But automated security details usually travelled in pairs in their allocated sectors, taking random streets so as to thwart any anticipation of their routes. Where there was one, there would be another.

Finn looked back to Jhara. The block she stood against was the last one before the edge of the dome. If she could get to the tunnel, Finn might be able to hide until the detail was gone. And if not... Finn swallowed her nervousness. Braithe had impressed upon her how important she, Finn, was to the mission. But better for Jhara to escape than have them both captured, interrogated, and sent to Central City.

Get to the tunnel! she mouthed at Jhara, pointing towards the dome wall. *Go now!*

Jhara's eyes were wide, her lips thin with worry.

Go now! Finn insisted, and Jhara turned and ran, long legs stretching out, feet landing quietly on the smooth path, almost silent strides and *fast.* Finn wished she had the same physical ability. She would have to rely on her wits instead.

There was a sound, a graze of metal on metal, Jhara had removed the vent cover. Finn held her breath. Jhara was being quiet and careful, but would the detail pick it up as a potential threat? Finn didn't dare look around the corner, and anyway, it was time for her to go. The detail's patrol partner could come down her street at any moment, and as much as she pressed against the wall, hidden by dark clothes in the darkness, her body heat signature would be a beacon to the detail's sensors.

Creeping back the way they had come, Finn made her way to the entrance of the accommodation block. Due to the careful monitoring by internal street cameras during the day, and the details at night, accommodation blocks were never locked, only those who needed to go in would go in. All Cityzens were afforded the same of everything – food, clothing, sparse furnishings. Theft was almost unheard of – why would anyone steal? Finn only knew of the concept through the lessons about the Badlanders and their reprehensible traits: violence, thievery, immorality.

Finn pressed her palm against the warmth of the bamboo frame and pushed very slowly. A tiny click, and the door opened, the pale light of the corridor a long thin rectangle on the step. Finn slipped inside, closing the door just as quietly, knowing that the sounds and the light would alert the details if they were close enough.

She knew better than to stay behind the door. A scan of the building would show an outline of her, crouched, as obvious as if she were standing in the middle of the street. Instead, she would have to seem as if she belonged.

Finn walked up the corridor and took the first turn to her left. Another long corridor stretched ahead, doors on both sides. She walked along it, and between the third and fourth door, stopped, calculated distance of the inner walls she could not see but which she knew were there. Then she sat on the floor, and lay down, as if asleep.

The accommodation block was silent, each room soundproofed from the others and the outside. Finn knew that there was no guarantee she would avoid the mobile security details when she left the building to join Jhara, but by counting the minutes, she could lower the risk. She concentrated on her breath, breathing away the panic, breathing in the calm. Just like Braithe had taught her.

She let the minutes pass.

Three.

Five.

Eight.

Time to go.

Finn stood and walked quickly back the way she had come. No point in delaying the inevitable. She had done everything possible, used all her knowledge. Now she just had to hope it was enough. She opened the door and slipped back into the dim night, her muscles tense.

The City was still. Any roaming details were too far away to hear, and Jhara's escape had obviously gone unnoticed, if the lack of personnel were anything to go by. All Finn had to do was to get to the tunnel.

She ran on light feet to the street where she and Jhara

had been separated. A quick glance both ways, and Finn followed the path Jhara had taken across the street, straight down the side of the block to the tunnel. By the time Finn reached the edge of the dome, her lungs clawed at her ribs with every breath, her legs shuddering with each step. She gasped for air, leaning over with her hands on her thighs, her vision dizzy.

The vent cover shifted slowly to the side and Finn saw Jhara's eyes in the darkness of the tunnel.

"Took your time," Jhara said, but her voice wobbled, and Finn knew it would have been a long ten minutes for her, too.

"Help me with this," said Jhara, sliding the cover over a little more. "I have to put it back after we're both in, so I need you to be in front. It'll probably be a bit less cramped for you, anyway."

Finn frowned, but when she bent down to look into the tunnel, she realised her height would indeed be an advantage. Jhara, over a head taller, would find it a tight fit.

"Still can't understand why they built the vents at the base of the dome rather than at the top," Finn said as she took her backpack from her shoulders, and helped lower the cover to the ground.

"Air is cleaner at ground level, and it's easier to maintain, Finn. You of all people should know."

"Still seems odd," Finn complained. "Surely it would cause more of a vacuum…"

She got down on hands and knees and Jhara got out. The vent cover was usually connected to an alarm, but it had been disabled through Finn's earlier work in the Ether. Once Jhara pulled it back over the tunnel, it would activate again within the hour, as if it had never been moved.

"You would do better to thank PlanetRescue for designing it this way," Jhara said, as Finn began to crawl forward, "or you'd be trying to get out through the skydome, and that'd be a long jump down."

It was dark inside the tunnel, but clean and smooth. Finn scrabbled to get her grip, but the pipe sloped downwards slightly, meaning that she only needed limited energy to keep moving at a steady pace. Jhara, catching her up, seemed to be finding it more difficult. Finn could see the end of the tunnel up ahead, another grill the only separation between them and the Badlands. Finn stopped moving suddenly, and a moment later Jhara bumped into her with a surprised grunt.

"What are you doing?" Jhara asked. "We need to keep

moving."

She was breathing heavily and Finn could feel the heat of her body next to hers.

Finn didn't answer, still looking at the grill.

"Ah," said Jhara, trying to shift into a more comfortable position. "Not talking."

She reached over to grab Finn's hand and Finn felt her fingers, warm and a bit sweaty, interlace with her own.

"We have been talking about this for months," said Jhara quietly.

Finn nodded in the darkness.

"Does it help if I remind you of that? And how much Braithe needs us to get to Seven Rivers? How important we both are?"

Finn nodded again.

"So we need to keep moving. And I will be with you all the way. It's us two, just like it has been all these years. What do we need the City for, right?"

Outside the City, there would be no World, Finn thought. There would be no easy connection between minds, no infinite colour or light or knowledge. There would be only what they could see or feel or hear around them, which seemed so limited and cumbersome, compared to the immersive experience of the World. Braithe had insisted that the Badlands were not the hellish carcinogenic environment that PlanetRescue had made them out to be, and Finn didn't have any reason not to believe her, but it was the unknown. Routine had been her comfort, if not her saviour, and this day was proving to be very much out of the ordinary, as would the following days. Finn felt the anxiety rising from her throat, and her head began to feel tight.

Jhara wrapped her arms around Finn's chest, holding her firmly against her body. Finn resisted, struggling against the close touch, her head feeling even more fragile, but after a few moments, she began to relax, her breathing slowing in time with Jhara's, the agitation retreating back inside her.

"Better?" asked Jhara, letting her go.

Finn breathed out slowly.

"Better."

"Then perhaps you'd like to kick this vent cover off and start this revolution properly?"

Finn smiled. Her panic had left her shaky but energised. She slid forward, pushing her regulation PlanetRescue clogs against the grill. Holding her breath, she shifted all her weight onto the grill and after a few seconds, metal screeched on metal and the cover fell the short distance onto the grey dirt of the Badlands.

They both jumped down, the landing sending a shock through their legs. Finn put her hands on the ground for balance. Grit pushed under her fingernails, and she felt the dust on her palms, as she touched the earth. It was unpleasant.

She breathed in the night air. It was pleasantly cool, but so different to the recycled air from the City. It almost had a taste to it, and it seemed strangely familiar. She couldn't decide whether she liked it or not, and took deep, careful breaths, trying to work out why she felt as if she had been here before.

The glow of the skydome behind them cast a soft light on the ground, but only a short distance away was darkness. Finn looked around, waiting for her eyes to adjust. The gentle hills spread out in front of them, pebbled and dry. There were some small plants, scrubby bushes and sparse grasses, but no trees. It really did look like the wastelands they'd been told about.

"Time to go, Finn," Jhara reminded her, brushing her

own hands on her thighs.

Finn sighed, but quietly. Only by going forwards would she be able to come back.

Chapter 2

It took some minutes for their muscles to warm up when they started jogging, but soon Finn found an easy rhythm. With Jhara keeping the pace ahead of her, Finn concentrated on her footfalls, watching the ground in front of her to avoid tussocks and rocks. They ran slowly, pacing themselves. Eventually, after almost an hour, Finn slowed to a walk and turned back to look at the City. They had been jogging up a slow incline and now they could see the skydome clearly down in the valley, as it shimmered where the moon reflected off its surface. Just to the north, three dozen or so windmills turned, their winged blades supplying power to the sleeping City.

"It looks so calm from out here, doesn't it?" Jhara said. "And Braithe is down there, gathering the troops... I hope she's OK."

She sat on the stony ground next to Finn and pushed her hair out of her eyes.

They sat and looked back at the City for a few moments in silence. The skydome was not quite opaque, so they could see the stumpy tower blocks, evenly spaced with narrow streets for the most efficient use of the area. Finn thought about all her colleagues still sleeping, and wondered about what might happen to them in the coming days, if the Revolution were really to begin. It suddenly occurred to her that PlanetRescue might be unwilling to give up any hold they had on the Cities. What would happen to the Cityzens? What might happen to Braithe and Jhara, and everyone who had been involved in this movement? Unlike the governments she had read about in the late twentieth and early twenty-first centuries, PlanetRescue didn't have to comply with any laws of democracy. As Braithe had taught her, they made the rules, and given the way the world was outside the Cities, few were going to question those rules. There had only been the failed Revolution years before, when Finn was just four years old. Much too young to remember it, or what had become of those who had been involved. She realised that Braithe had never really mentioned that, either.

Jhara stood up and stretched, and held her hand out for Finn to pull herself to her feet.

"Let's run for a bit longer. Then we can walk for a while."

They started off again, the terrain steeper and more

uneven than before. Finn's feet began to rub against her thin clogs, a dull pain that steadily got worse. After only a short distance, she began to walk. Jhara was still running, and turned when she discovered Finn was no longer beside her.

"You can't?" she asked.

Finn shook her head, and Jhara sighed.

"We really could have done with more training," she said, sounding resigned for the first time. "I don't even know how far we've got to go."

"I just need to sit for a while."

Finn half-fell onto her knees and one elbow as she tried to lower herself to the ground, and Jhara dropped her backpack down to sit beside her. Everything hurt: her body, her head, her eyes. Braithe had done her best to prepare her but the Badlands had sharp edges, sharp smells. The entire environment poked at her senses.

"Let's see what Braithe has packed to eat. We would have had our breakfast by now, probably."

Jhara felt around inside the bag and Finn looked up at the sky. Directly above them it was a deep black-blue, speckled with stars, but towards the horizon, the colours were starting to change. The pictures of sunrises she had seen inWorld were gaudily bright, but seeing the real thing was unexpectedly moving. She felt a shiver run over her skin, despite not feeling cold.

"Here," said Jhara, throwing a wrapped parcel to her. "I think Braithe has been stealing rations for us... What kind of role model is she? I'll grow up delinquent. No wonder PlanetRescue mandates company-controlled parenting."

Finn smiled and opened the parcel. It was a breakfast ration, just the usual vegetable filling wrapped in an algae sheet, but somehow it tasted different, as they sat in the open air, looking at the rising sun.

"You don't think we need to worry about radiation?" Finn said.

They looked around as the early morning light cast shadows across the hill, highlighting the pebbles and rocks.

"I guess worrying won't do any good," Jhara said. "We're here now. But I suppose I would have expected some kind of sign..."

"You don't," said Finn. "Not unless it's really bad. You get sick later. Sometimes it's months later, and then they can't make you better, not really. There's –"

"Well, we're out here and there's nothing we can do

about it," repeated Jhara firmly. "Let's just hope it's all a myth. Braithe said as much, and since Serena and the rest of them in Seven Rivers have lived out here for decades, I'm sure she's right."

Finn nodded and took another bite of the ration. She wasn't convinced, but she sensed that Jhara didn't want to discuss it any more. Over in the east, the sky brightened and Finn felt the gentle heat on her hands and face.

"We should get on," said Jhara.

She handed Finn a water ration, and Finn put the rubbery bauble into her mouth, popping it with her tongue. The water spread out around her teeth and she swallowed it, then pulled out the remains of the seaweed skin which had held the water. She flicked it away onto the dry ground.

"Everyone else just eats the skin," said Jhara, tying up the backpack.

"I'm not everyone else," shrugged Finn. "The texture is weird."

Jhara closed her eyes and sighed.

"Let's just get going," she said.

They both stood, slowly, and Finn groaned softly as she felt the discomfort in her feet and legs even more, now they had rested. They had at least a day ahead of them. They hoisted their packs onto their shoulders and began to walk towards the sun.

"Ready?" Jhara asked.

And without waiting for Finn to answer, she turned and set off to the east. Finn pulled the straps on her backpack tighter and followed on behind.

~~~~~

The day passed slowly. The monotony of each step was only offset by the pain Finn felt every time she put a foot to the ground. The surface changed from the hard stones where they had breakfasted, to a soft sand, but each was as difficult to navigate as the other. The sun rose steadily in a cloudless sky. By mid-morning, they had reached the edge of the forest Braithe had mentioned, and the shade and cool air were welcome, even if the twigs and leaves slowed down their pace. Once they had walked far enough that they could only see forest in every direction, they stopped to rest, their eyes having adjusted to the filtered light.

"I feel safer here," said Finn, sitting on the ground and
~~~~~

examining a tiny sapling. "I know they have the ability to find us anywhere, but I still feel better now we're in among all this other life."

"They'd also have to get to us," Jhara said. "At least all these trees makes that harder."

Neither spoke for a few minutes. The forest had been quiet when they first entered it, but Finn realised that this was probably due to their own noise. Now that they had stopped walking, the birds and other creatures moved about, still unseen but calling out, perhaps reassuring themselves that these loud strangers were nothing to be feared. Being around such a lot of green plant life was calming. The air smelt different, too. Finn gently rubbed her hand along the rough bark of a tree trunk, feeling the uneven grooves and lumps. Such asymmetry.

"We should keep moving," she said, even though her body ached at the thought.

Jhara looked just as unenthusiastic, but agreed. She stood and rubbed her hands on the front of her PlanetRescue leggings.

"I think I can hear water," she said. "Maybe over this way? That'll be the creek we need to follow. It comes off the

Seven Rivers."

Finn walked ahead, pushing branches carefully so they wouldn't fling back to hit Jhara behind her. It took longer than they expected, but eventually they discovered a small path which led along the steep bank of a creek. The sound of water running across rocks and half-submerged branches was calming. Finn tried to focus on the music of it, rather than her own exhaustion. Behind her, she heard Jhara stumble. Finn turned just in time to see her fall backwards down the bank, landing on rocks and branches.

Jhara's face contorted, creased with silent agony, as if the fall had knocked all the sound from her body. Finn couldn't understand how only a few seconds could wreak such an injury; her eyes were drawn to Jhara's leg, the ugliness of split skin and bone and blood.

Finn scrabbled down the bank and knelt down next to Jhara, trying to think of something to say. She glanced at the wound and winced, her stomach squeezing into a ball.

"I can't... what..."

Jhara was holding her breath, her skin suddenly many shades paler than usual.

"Oh, Jhara... oh..."

Finn leant forward to touch her, but then pulled back, unsure of what she could do without causing more pain. Jhara was lying in an awkward position but seemed too rigid to move. Finn closed her eyes and breathed, trying to stop the sound of her own blood in her ears which was making her head tight. Next to her, Jhara moaned, and then was silent.

She wasn't sure how long she sat with her eyes closed, but she opened them immediately when she felt a hand on her arm. Expecting Jhara, she gasped and fell onto her side when she saw another person sitting next to her, touching her gently. She opened her mouth to scream, but instead simply looked from the new person, to Jhara, and all around the forest, wondering if there were others, hiding.

"Finn..."

He knew her name.

She looked at him, trying to decide if they had met before. He was a bit older than she was, she guessed. His hair hung in loose curls around his face. He smiled a quick smile, blue eyes crinkling at the edges.

"I'm Toby," he said, and then looked down at Jhara. "She's badly hurt. I wish I could have found you both earlier.

We knew you were coming, but..."

He did seem genuinely sorry. Finn stared at him for a few seconds. She shook her head, looking at Jhara and trying to clear her mind. If she trusted this Toby, then Jhara might be safe. If she didn't trust him, Jhara might die. She couldn't leave Jhara, and Toby had found them without being seen. There was no escape.

"OK. You need to help her, then," she said, briefly making eye contact.

Toby rubbed his thumb along his lips.

"I don't know if we can move her in the truck," he said. "Let me call Serena."

Serena.

Finn looked around. Braithe had told them so much about her, she found herself both excited and terrified at the thought of meeting her. Toby put two fingers in his mouth and blew, the sharp whistle shrieking around the forest, bouncing off trees and sending birds fleeing for safety. Finn wished she could fly away, too. Some moments passed in silence, and then a tall woman, with long dark hair with several wisps of grey, stepped carefully through bushes and over fallen branches to where Finn and Toby stood.

She put her hand out to Finn and they pressed palms, in the traditional City greeting.

"Finn," she said. She had dark, serious eyes and she stared hard at Finn, but her voice was deep and gentle. "It's good to see you again. We came looking for you as soon as we heard you were coming."

She knelt down next to Jhara, putting a soft hand on her forehead, and looked back to Toby.

"She's in shock," she said. There was no fear in her voice, but it was obvious that she was concerned. Finn studied her face, creased in well-worn lines, a face that had practised the full spectrum of emotions.

"We need to get her to Seven Rivers straight away. What do you have in the first aid kit?"

Toby shrugged, and listed a few words which Finn didn't recognise. Serena nodded, and began to give both of them instructions: Finn to fetch branches, Toby to retrieve the equipment from the truck. It was a relief to have someone who seemed comfortable with the surroundings, and with being in charge. Finn did as she was told. Serena, meanwhile, sat next to Jhara, whose eyes remained closed, skin pale as the moon.

Finn focused on the tasks she was given, but her mind was a tumult of questions. Serena was here instead of at Seven Rivers, where they had expected to find her. She had met Finn before even though Finn didn't remember either her or Toby. The awkward newness of everything knotted itself around her chest.

Serena and Toby worked to put together a makeshift stretcher, and Serena mixed some medicine together from the small bottles Toby had brought from the truck. She murmured something to Jhara, who obediently opened her mouth and allowed Serena to rub the preparation on her gums. After a few moments, Jhara's expression relaxed, and her breathing slowed, but was more even.

"She's comfortable, now," said Serena, "and we can move her without putting her through pain. I'll need your help, both of you."

Jhara weighed far more than Finn could have imagined, and even though the truck was parked on an old track only a few minutes' walk away, she felt as if her arms were slowly being torn from her body. It was hard not to trip on the plants and exposed roots on the forest floor.

By the time they had loaded the stretcher onto the back

and tied it down, Finn was barely able to stand. Serena noticed, and helped her into the cab. Finn tried to identify the smell. People, some kind of perfume? And dirt and leaves, like the forest? The City autodrivers were always clinically odourless. She held her breath for a moment, but it wasn't long before she got used to it. It wasn't unpleasant as it was simply noticeable, just another mark of difference.

"I'll be in the back with Jhara," Serena said. "Rest as much as you can. It will be a few hours before we get home."

Home.

Finn closed her eyes.

Chapter 3

The sun was beginning to set when Finn woke, as the truck ground through gears and shuddered to a stop. For a moment, she wasn't sure exactly where she was. She glanced over and saw Toby, who had opened the door and was halfway out of it.

"Well, we're here," he said, holding onto a handle on the outside of the truck and leaning out from the step. "Welcome to Seven Rivers."

In the late afternoon light, the settlement looked mythic. From the tall eucalypts in the west, shadows drooled lazily over small houses and orange warmth stretched into the gaps between.

"I'm just getting some help for Jhara," said Toby.

He seemed more relaxed, happy to be back. He jumped down onto the dirt road and closed the truck door firmly. Finn watched as he jogged down the road in front of the truck. There were others walking around, carrying baskets, or cycling on bicycles. She couldn't see any other vehicles.

It was only a few minutes before he came back with three others, a woman slightly older than he was, and two younger men. They were talking animatedly, obviously pleased to see Toby. This kind of easy company didn't happen in the City, especially not for Finn.

There was a tap at the window and Finn looked down to see Serena standing next to the truck. She smiled at Finn and reached up to open the door.

"You might feel a bit sore," she said. "You're not used to the walking, and it's been a difficult day. Is it OK for me to help you down?"

Finn nodded, not thinking until her feet touched the ground that it was odd to be asked. Braithe and Jhara knew about her dislike of close touch, but for Serena to know? It was yet another unanswered question.

Around the back of the truck, Toby and his friends were carefully lifting Jhara off, still strapped to her stretcher, eyes closed, and quiet. Finn noticed that her leg had been bandaged, and someone had laid a jacket over her chest and arms.

"Come on," said Serena, pointing at one of the houses. "Let's get you inside so you can have something to eat."

They stepped into cool shadow, and onto the soft dirt at the side of the road. Serena led Finn up the steps, into the wooden house. Inside, it smelt like someone had been cooking.

Serena pulled out a seat for Finn, and filled a kettle. So much of this Finn had only seen inWorld; it was strange to watch someone carry out such basic and antiquated tasks. Serena was silent as she put the kettle on a wood-fired stove, and then took some kind of food out of a cupboard, and set about preparing it. The silence was not uncomfortable, and Finn felt reluctant to break it, but she was concerned.

"Where is Jhara?" she asked, her voice suddenly loud in the quiet.

Serena stopped cutting, and looked over at Finn.

"Sorry, I should have said. She's with some of the others. Being cared for. She won't wake for several hours, most likely. Her body needs to rest, and heal. They'll take care of her. You don't have to worry."

Finn nodded. Serena seemed to realise her concern, and smiled.

"You are safe, here," she said, gently. "We're chasing the same thing, we've been working towards the same thing. It'll be some days, even a week or so. But we'll head back to the City, all of us. Soon."

Finn wondered if Serena could sense her impatience.

"For now, you need to eat, and then we can talk a bit. I'm sure you have some questions. After you've rested, Jhara might be awake, too. And you can both see each other again."

Finn weighed up the situation. Serena knew such a lot about them; Braithe had insisted that she was to be trusted. There was no way for Finn to get back to the City yet, and she couldn't leave Jhara. As uncomfortable as she felt, she knew that this was as safe a place as any.

"This'll take a while," Serena continued, motioning at the food with her knife. "Why don't I show you where you can wash?"

Finn rose, gingerly putting her weight on her tender feet, and followed Serena down a short hallway. There was a bedroom at the end. Finn noticed two beds made up with chaotically colourful patchwork quilts.

"You'll sleep in there," Serena said, then moved to the left of the room, and into a small but clean bathroom. The floor was made from wood, just like the rest of the house, but it was shiny and smoother. Serena put the plug in the bath and started running the water. She showed Finn how to adjust and turn off the taps.

"Don't make it too deep," she said. "We have a lot of water right now, but that can always change. It's not easy to anticipate the weather nowadays, not for a long time. I suppose you don't have that problem in the City."

She smiled, but Finn couldn't think of anything to say, so she stayed silent.

"Well, I'll be in the kitchen," said Serena. "Take as long as you need. There are towels here, and oh –"

She raised a finger, and walked back past Finn, returning a few seconds later with some folded clothes.

"We thought you'd probably like to change," she said, simply. She left them on a small wooden stool next to the basin, and closed the door quietly.

With the water running steadily into the bath, Finn took her time undressing. Her arms and legs felt heavy, and only when she peeled off the last piece of PlanetRescue clothing did she realise how dirty and sweaty she had become. She stepped into the warm bath struggling with the sensation of being enveloped in an unfamiliar medium. She knew about the concept of baths from history lessons, but the reality was hard to describe. It took a long time to relax, but the heat of the water and the steam which rose from it were soporific and Finn leant her head on the cool enamel at the end of the tub and closed her eyes. Despite having slept for several hours in the truck, she still felt an exhaustion like she had never experienced. She dozed, her mind drifting in and out of sleep, instinctively wanting to connect inWorld, and feeling the loss of it when she couldn't.

Eventually, the water cooled and Finn dried herself and dressed in the clothing Serena had brought in for her. The long pants had been mended and patched, and the undershirt was knitted from a furry, lumpy fabric. It was looser than the uniform she had worn in the City, and had been worn many times before by someone else. Still, it was warm and soft.

There was a gentle knock at the door.

"We have some food ready, if you're up to it?"

Finn opened the door and Serena seemed surprised.

"Ah, you're dressed! I'm glad we got the sizes fairly right. Hard to tell at short notice. Come on. Toby is just about finished making dinner, and some of the others are here. Everyone's very excited to see you."

Finn followed her back through the house, towards the

mumble of noise in the kitchen. When they got there, she stayed in the hallway, while Serena strolled through the middle of the group, smiling and nodding. She stood at the end of the table and nodded to Finn, and to the others in the room, who gradually stopped talking.

"It's good of you all to come," said Serena. "As you can see, Finn has arrived. With Jhara, who unfortunately can't be here at this moment."

Most of the faces turned to see Finn, and some smiled at her. Finn wasn't sure which expression was appropriate, so she looked at the floor. Serena continued.

"This is short notice, I know. But we have been preparing for this for years. It shouldn't come as a surprise. We plan to attack as soon as we can be ready."

There was a low murmuring – Finn looked around the room and noticed Toby standing to the side of the kitchen bench. The rest of them, Finn didn't recognise. Her thoughts went to Jhara. She wished she had been able to see her instead of having to stand in a room full of strangers. But for now, she had to take Serena's word that Jhara was still sleeping. It was true that they both needed to rest.

"We all know our tasks," said Serena. "I'll be coordinating

from here, as is the plan. At the moment we're stuck without any contact with our friends in other Cities. We knew that this would happen and it's why we needed Finn and Jhara. We have to assume that we're running on the same timetable and hope that we can liaise as planned."

This time, there was no murmuring. Serena continued.

"We may not get this chance again. I wouldn't ask this of you if it weren't necessary."

This was very similar to what Braithe had said, Finn remembered. She wondered about the two of them. How did she and Braithe know each other? It was illegal to leave the City and there was no way that Serena, a Badlander, would have been allowed in. She wondered if Serena might tell her later, if she asked.

"That said," Serena went on, "I'm sure many of you will be keen to get moving straight away. But we need to be as prepared as possible, and that means having everyone at full strength."

Another brief pause.

"That's all for now," Serena said. "I'll be checking in with Elders again tomorrow."

Everyone began to chat among themselves as they

slowly moved out of the kitchen back into the night. Finn noticed how many different people there were – different sizes, different skin colours, many of them older than she'd ever seen. So unlike the City.

Serena walked over to Finn.

"How are you feeling?"

Finn shrugged.

"Less sore," she said. "Hungry, I suppose."

"I'm glad to hear it. We were looking forward to having a meal with you."

She offered Finn a chair, and took some plates from shelves at the back wall. Toby placed a steaming pot on the table, and began to ladle a stew onto the plates.

"I hope you like it," he said to Finn. "It's probably nothing like you're used to in the City, but it's one of my favourites."

"No pressure, though," said Serena, with a small laugh, as she nudged Toby in the ribs.

"Yeah. It's fine. I can take the criticism."

Finn smiled, too, although the exchange between them did nothing to make her feel more included. If anything she wished more than ever that she were back in the City. She raised the fork to her mouth, and tasted the stew.

It was rich and fragrant, with several different flavours. At first, it was overpowering, but slowly, as if her mind were catching up with the new experience, she chewed and swallowed, and realised how hungry she was, not just for food, but for this food.

"So I guess it's not too bad?" Toby asked, dimples showing as she quickly took two more mouthfuls.

"Shh, Toby. You'll embarrass her. Let's just eat."

They all ate quickly, and Finn felt satisfied and warm afterwards. The food she had eaten all her life was nothing compared to this. Toby took her plate when she was done, and began washing up.

"I'm only doing this because it's a special occasion, Finn," he said. "You realise that the rule is if you cook, you don't have to do the dishes."

"Stop your complaining. You've got a way to go before we're even with the dishes," said Serena, standing, and pushing in her chair.

She seemed stern, but when Finn looked over at her, she winked.

"Come on, Finn. I want to show you something."

Serena held her arm out for Finn, so she could lean on

her when she got up.

"We need to take a little walk," she said.

She slipped some soft shoes on which she had left near the door, and pointed out a pair that Finn could wear.

"Your PlanetRescue clogs are almost worn through. They can't stand up to the Badlands! You can have those ones."

They headed out the kitchen door, where the guests had left an hour before. The dark felt heavy and damp, but all around were the warm lights of other houses, and Finn enjoyed the sense of sinking into the dirt as they walked.

"It's not far," said Serena. "Oh, and just over there, that's where Jhara is sleeping. Eleanor is looking after her, and she'll come and get me as soon as she wakes, even if it's during the night. I don't think she'll wake before morning, but still."

They walked slowly, Finn leaning on the older woman for support. Serena's hands were cool, and Finn noticed again the smell of her, just as she had noticed it with Toby and the others who had been in the kitchen: a warm scent, like food and plants. She wondered if this was just how people were supposed to smell, when they weren't in such a sterile environment as the City.

"Here we are. See? Not far at all."

Serena pointed to a small house, similar in build to all the others: raised off the ground on short stilts, with wooden steps leading up to a front door. Unlike most of the others, this house was in darkness – no yellow light spilling out from its windows onto the ground below.

"This house, Finn," said Serena, stopping at the bottom of the steps and grabbing Finn's hand, "is where you were born."

Finn felt her mouth open slowly in surprise.

"Born..."

"Seven Rivers is your home," said Serena. "You and your parents lived here for two years before they died. Some of the Elders decided that it would be best if you were to grow up in the City, and Braithe agreed to take you and Jhara and beg to be let in as refugees. The City was doing that, back then."

"Why... how did they...? Why couldn't I stay?"

Finn felt the questions lining themselves up, filling her mouth and throat with confusion.

"Let's sit," said Serena, and they sat on the steps. The

wood was cool and smooth on Finn's palms as she lowered herself onto it.

"You know that years ago, we in the Badlands tried to get rid of PlanetRescue, and that we failed. We had to withdraw and there were heavy losses... PlanetRescue killed many of our people. It was an unfair fight, and we were foolish to have started it."

Finn nodded. She wanted badly to interrupt – this was not giving her the answers she needed.

"But it didn't change how we felt about PlanetRescue. We knew they had lied about the numbers of people they had allowed into their Cities. We knew they were holding governments to ransom. A new governor had taken over – Eva – and she was cruel as she was greedy. The Cities seemed to have no place for any of us who were too old, too disabled, or too darkly coloured."

Finn looked at Serena.

"They shut you out, from the start," she said, matter-of-factly.

"Yes, they did. Or rounded so many up, sending them who knows where. And of course, they had their special domes and their water purifiers, and their food manufacturing plants, and we had the dirt and the sun."

She sighed, her elbows on her knees, leaning forward so that her shoulders hunched and Finn could no longer clearly see her face.

"The radiation was a lie. There was only ever some residue from the chemical mixture they'd used to seed the clouds, to get it to rain. Whatever it was. And some of us got sick, but we recovered, and we started over."

She stood up, almost agitated, Finn thought.

"You've seen who we are. We're the ones they left out. But they had no idea about our history. We came together to share all our histories, used our collective experience, used the knowledge of all our cultures. We survived."

She stopped and looked back. Finn found it hard to read her expression.

"And my parents..." Finn prompted her.

"Yes. Sorry. Of course, your parents."

Serena came back to sit next to Finn, her sadness and anger visibly dissipating. She seemed keen to talk about them.

"They were very involved in the Revolution. They believed that we needed to get rid of PlanetRescue; they didn't trust them."

"But you decided that I should live in a PlanetRescue City?" Finn said, suspiciously.

"I understand that sounds strange. But we had a plan in place. Your parents were high-level targets. PlanetRescue was working to root out the troublemakers, and their methods were brutal… we needed to keep you safe. Braithe volunteered to go in, and take you and Jhara, so she could keep watch over you, and also organise the resistance from the inside. It was risky, definitely. But the Elders took a long time over it, and thought it would be the best way."

"Hiding in plain sight."

"Exactly. We knew you were different, and that it might be hard for you in the City. We worried. They were very strict in who they allowed to live there – the brightest, the fittest."

Finn frowned, the questions not quite formed in her mind.

"We knew you could be on the inside without attracting too much attention. PlanetRescue was known for choosing the Cityzens very… carefully," Serena continued. "Braithe could offer intel on us. She gave them enough so they thought they were in control. But she was our contact.

Working for us – for this. You being here. The takedown."

They were both quiet for a few moments.

"So now," said Finn, "you are planning to attack PlanetRescue again. Why do it again, given the results last time?"

Serena smiled.

"This time, we have you."

Finn gave her a sharp look, then realised that might seem rude. Serena, however, didn't seem to notice.

"This time, it's bigger. It's global. There are Resistance all over the world. Once we succeed here, they will know. It will give them the power. The whole system will fall."

"That is a big… thing," said Finn.

"Yes, it is. And now you understand. We can't fail."

Finn put her hands back on the smooth steps, feeling the lines where the dirt had seeped in. She rubbed her fingers back and forth, imagining the age of the wood, the tree it had come from, the feet and shoes which had walked up and down. Anything to escape the enormity of the plan that Serena had just described.

Chapter 4

Finn woke early the next morning, when the sky was still grey, but already there were noises from the kitchen – people talking, plates and cups being moved about. Not excited about the idea of being sociable so early in the morning, Finn instead walked over to the window and looked out over the town. Serena and Toby's house was on a hill, so she could see about two dozen houses spread out down the gentle slope towards the bottom of the valley. A creek – a river, really – was just visible in the distance. Along one side of the hill, and up on the top of the other side of the valley, were rows of tall windmills, their wooden wings carved and smooth as they swung gently, round and round. The motion was mesmerising, and Finn watched for a while as the sun came up, somewhere behind her, and spread out across the town and the landscape beyond. Across on the other side of the valley, a group of kangaroos were hunched over, feeding on the grass.

There was so much space. The dome which covered the City was unobtrusive, letting in sunlight and a hint of the blue sky, so much that it didn't quite feel like a barrier, but a membrane, protecting them. But here the horizon seemed to move even further away as she looked at it, and left Finn with a longing for more.

She watched as the people below began to move about outside their homes. Some wandered about their gardens, harvesting fruit or herbs, others simply sat on the steps, drinking from mugs. Some were feeding birds which had flown down from the grove of eucalypts Finn had seen the day before. Everyone seemed to be enjoying the sunshine, and the quiet. Finn wondered if her parents had also sat on the steps of their house, and she thought about the conversation she had had with Serena the night before. They had walked back to Serena's house, mostly in silence, as Finn had processed what Serena had told her. Once back inside, Toby had made tea and then he and Serena had talked about PlanetRescue's history: how the cloud-seeding PlanetRescue had sold governments had caused flooding and mass casualties; how there was suspicion about the radiation levels but PlanetRescue insisted that they were dangerously high; how PlanetRescue had convinced heads of state everywhere that their domed Cities were the only safe refuge but had then charged governments for their use;

how PlanetRescue had slowly and insidiously, become a de facto, international ruling force. But they were simply words. Finn found herself just returning to the idea of living in Seven Rivers, and having parents. Even though she'd heard some of this information before, from Braithe and from her own research inWorld, and she knew how much it mattered, all she could focus on was her past.

There was a knock at the door and Finn turned around, but nobody came in.

"Finn?" asked Serena, through the door after a moment's silence.

"Yes?"

"Can I come in?"

"Oh. Yes!"

Finn blushed, walking towards the door; Serena opened it and poked her head into the room.

"Would you like some breakfast?"

Finn nodded, still thinking of the people she had just seen out of the window, and wondering how many of them had been involved in the last Revolution. How many of them had planned and engaged alongside her parents?

"You can eat in the garden, if you like," Serena was

saying as Finn dragged her concentration back to the present. "There are some people in the kitchen who would like to talk with you, but I get it if you don't feel like you can be in there with them just yet."

"I'd prefer to be alone," said Finn.

Serena nodded, and they walked through to the kitchen, where she handed Finn some of the bread – damper, she remembered them calling it.

"Enjoy the fresh air," Serena said, with a smile.

Outside, it was cooler, and Finn was grateful of the layers of clothing she was wearing, although she missed the close fit of the regulation issue pants, shirts and jacket which she had been used to in the City. These still felt like someone else's clothes, in someone else's home. She laughed at herself – homesick for the City. She bit into a piece of the damper, warm and with some other flavour – garlic, Serena had said – which was both sharp and fragrant. As she chewed, she tried to think about how she might have turned out, if she had grown up here. She would still have known Jhara. Braithe would have looked after her, possibly Serena, too. There seemed to be an acceptance here which didn't exist in the City, simply the variety in the people pointed to this. Perhaps life would have been easier, if she had been allowed to stay?

Finn sighed. The anger creeping into her forehead was pointless, and she breathed, slowly, in an attempt to calm herself. It was in the past, and had always been out of her hands. She could acknowledge the emotion, but holding onto it would only cause her anguish. Gradually, the irritation subsided, and she continued to eat her food. She smiled a small smile. Braithe would be proud of her. The training had paid off.

"Tea?"

Finn jumped and turned to see Toby standing on the steps, two mugs in hand.

"Oh! Please," she said, holding out her hand to take one. "I didn't hear you."

"I'm very quiet," he shrugged, and sat down on a large section of tree trunk, the top of which had been smoothed and polished.

"How are you getting on, then?" he asked.

"I'm… it's different."

"I can imagine."

Finn drank her tea and tried to think of something to say,

but Toby spoke first.

"Serena asked if I could take you over to see Jhara. She's awake, and feeling much better. Would you like to go?"

"Yes! Yes, I would like that."

"Well, you can bring your tea, if you like. It's just over on the other side of the road and a few houses down."

They stood, the sun bright on their faces as they moved out of the shadows of the fruit trees and berry bushes. Holding the tea so she wouldn't spill it took more concentration than Finn expected, so it took them several minutes to get to the house. Toby opened a small gate, motioning for Finn to hurry through. Once inside the gate, Finn saw the reason for the urgency: two young dogs came running towards them, a chaos of legs and floppy ears and tongues. Finn held her mug against her chest, took a frantic, tense breath, and backed against the garden fence and the leaves of the tree which grew beside it.

"Boys!" said Toby.

He was attempting to be stern, but his obvious amusement at Finn's discomfort gave him away, and the dogs ignored him, jumping up at Finn and panting delightedly. Finn held her breath and her tea, terrified. After several seconds of this, a sharp whistle from the inside of the house caught the immediate attention of the pups, who bounded together back to the steps of the house. Finn exhaled slowly.

"I forgot you weren't used to animals," Toby said, by way of apology.

Finn shrugged, hoping it wouldn't be apparent how unsettling it had been, and followed Toby into the house, where the dogs were nowhere to be seen. Presumably, the owner of the whistle had shut them away in another room, because inside, it was dim and quiet. The curtains were drawn, and the creaking of the floorboards underfoot was the only sound.

"Through here," Toby said softly, and pointed to a room off the kitchen. The house was a similar layout to Serena's, Finn thought, and she wondered if all the houses in Seven Rivers might have been made to the same plan. The efficiency of that idea appealed to her.

Toby knocked gently on the door and someone murmured something from the other side, and then opened it and looked at them both.

"You must be Finn," she said, holding out her palm to

press against Finn's. "I'm Eleanor. I guess you'd like to see the patient?"

She was perhaps about Serena and Braithe's age, with kind blue eyes and greying hair cut short. She smelt like something green and fresh, and seemed very comfortable with the idea of people simply walking into her house.

Eleanor stepped aside and they walked into the room, which was brighter than the rest of the house, the curtains drawn back to let in some of the morning light. On a bed next to the far wall, Jhara lay, her leg bandaged with a less rudimentary splint, and her torso propped up on pillows. Finn smiled, warm relief spreading through her chest.

"Hey, lazy butt," said Jhara, still looking tired and pale, but smiling deeply enough that her dimples showed. "Took your time to come and see me."

"Who's lazy?" asked Finn, trying to keep the laugh out of her voice. "I've been exploring the neighbourhood and was attacked by wild dogs!"

"Ah, the puppies," said Eleanor. "I'm so sorry. Ian has taken care of them, I hope. They're in need of training."

"We're not so used to animals," Jhara explained.

"I know," Eleanor said. "There is a lot for you to get used

to, now."

She paused and looked at them all, and something – a question, maybe? – hung in the air, before Eleanor changed the subject.

"Shall I get you some more tea?"

She held out her hand for Finn and Toby's mugs. Finn was about to refuse, but Toby accepted and offered to help Eleanor make it. They left the room, and Finn could hear them talking as they walked into the kitchen together.

"So how are you?" asked Jhara. She pressed her lips together as she shifted her weight in the bed, the discomfort obvious.

"Me? I'm fine," said Finn, shrugging, and then remembered her conversation with Serena the night before. "Did you know about us, then? That we're from here?"

Jhara nodded.

"Braithe told me a few months ago, when we were getting ready."

"And you didn't tell me?"

Jhara didn't speak for a moment, taking her time to study Finn's face.

"It was at Braithe's insistence. I didn't like the idea of

keeping secrets. Are you upset?"

Finn took a breath and thought about her answer.

"No..." she said, slowly. "I'm... surprised. Not so much because you two didn't tell me. More because I didn't even consider the possibility of it. I have no memories of here. Do you?"

Jhara shrugged.

"A few? I guess only once Braithe reminded me. You were a lot younger, you know. Those five years between us made a difference at that age."

"I'm also not sure what they expect of me," Finn continued. "Serena has been happy to answer questions about my past but we haven't discussed what role I'm going to play in this attack. I know Braithe wouldn't have sent us here without good reason, but I worry about whether... it has been a long time since she was in the Badlands. Maybe things are different to what she remembers."

"It's natural to be confused," Jhara reassured her. "I know, I can imagine your reservations. I know you don't like change. Eleanor hasn't said anything either, but I don't know if there's anything sinister going on."

"Maybe all this stuff we've learnt about PlanetRescue in

the past months has made me more suspicious than usual," Finn smiled.

"Than usual?" laughed Jhara. "Like you ever were! Braithe had to spend hours talking to you and showing you proof of PlanetRescue's duplicity. Proof of the acid rain *and* the flooding, proof that they were using human bodies in Central City for fuel..."

Jhara stopped. She had been joking and these weren't revelations to either of them anymore, but thinking too hard about them was confronting.

"Nothing wrong with wanting proof..." Finn knew she sounded defensive.

"No, but your requirements are maybe a bit more excessive than the average person."

Finn shrugged and Jhara gave her a gentle shove.

"It's good that you're thinking more critically," Jhara said, gently. "But just relax. We have... what, a couple of days? I don't know what's going to happen, but obviously I won't be walking anywhere. The medicines Serena gave me in the forest worked well, but I won't be able to walk the same for weeks."

Finn suddenly felt hollow.

"But what... this is exactly why I'm so worried! What is going to happen? How are they going to organise an attack? It all seems so unclear!"

"Ah, but Serena has a plan," Eleanor said from behind her.

Finn startled and turned around to see Toby and Eleanor coming through the doorway with the tea. They set the mugs down on the bedside table, and Eleanor pointed to two wooden chairs in the far corner, which Finn had not noticed before. She took her mug with a nod, and sat on one of the chairs.

"We have been looking forward to this day for a long time," Eleanor said. "It must seem strange to you, but before we finally lost regular signal, we'd been in contact with Braithe and others in the Resistance in the City for years. And you're both important – we wouldn't be able to succeed in this final stage without you."

"You're not going to sacrifice us, are you?" asked Finn.

Eleanor threw her head back and laughed, almost spilling her tea. It took her a moment to recover and speak.

"No!" she said, still smiling, when the chuckles had subsided. "No, we aren't. Where did you get such an idea?"

Jhara smiled.

"Finn's thoughts don't always follow the same path as the rest of us," she said, simply.

"I know this has been confusing," said Eleanor. "Jhara can get up and move around today, though. So perhaps you can explore the community for a couple of hours this morning, and then this afternoon when we have our meeting, there'll be more information. I think it will all be a bit clearer to you then."

Finn drank some tea. It was hot and sweet.

"No human sacrifices, I promise," Eleanor added, her bright eyes twinkling.

Jhara had not yet been up on her feet since the fall, so helping her upright took a little time and the efforts of Toby, Eleanor and Finn combined. Finn could see Jhara turning pale. Eleanor noticed as well, and put a calming hand on Jhara's cheek.

"It will hurt only a little, I know how to set bones, and you have crutches here, and we will not let you fall."

Jhara smiled a strained smile, and nodded. She held her breath, and pulled her weight up onto her good leg.

"Huh," she said. "You're right. It's... OK."

Eleanor made sure she was balanced and let Finn and Toby hold her steady while she picked up the crutches that had been propped up against the wall.

"Try these... that's it... under your arms. I understand that it will feel a little odd."

Shifting her torso around to find a comfortable place for the pads under her arms, Jhara finally nodded, and Finn and Toby carefully let go and stepped to the side.

"It's OK," Jhara said again, more sure of herself this time. "I can do it. Wow... what a strange sensation."

Eleanor smiled.

"It's not something you would ever have seen before, I imagine," she said. "Or if so, then only inWorld."

She sighed.

"Oh, with all that has happened in that City, and others like it..." she looked at all of them, her expression one of sadness and perhaps regret.

"But!" she continued, more brightly. "Hopefully this will all change. Well, that's the plan, yes?"

Finn suspected her change in mood was an attempt to steering them away from either questioning what she had meant, or dwelling on the fact that if Jhara had been so badly injured in the City, then she would not have been allowed to stay.

Outside in the daylight, Jhara made slow progress, and at first, Finn watched her carefully, concerned that she might lose her balance. But Jhara had a natural athleticism which apparently extended to using these walking aids, and after a few moments, she began to gain confidence and seemed very sturdy. Finn relaxed and began to take in the surroundings. In the bright day, she could see the small details she'd missed the previous night – how every house had its own water tank, and large rectangular solar panels on the rooves. All houses were raised up off the ground, with wooden steps leading up to the front doors. Like the blocks in the City, here the buildings were obviously made from whatever materials were at hand. But here they were more varied, somehow sturdier with rougher edges. Corrugated iron, brick, wood, all carefully put together to make a solid shelter.

The ground began to slope gently downwards and Finn realised they were heading towards the river.

"This is where all seven rivers converge," Toby said, as he lengthened his stride and walked down to the bank. "Up there, you can see them coming in, or at least, two of them. They sort of join in at different spots. When you're able, we can go on a hike up there, maybe."

Finn smiled and nodded non-committedly, but wondered about this vague discussion of the future. She knew the next couple of days would be the decider as to whether they'd even be able to continue living out there. How could Toby even imagine what was going to happen after that?

Down by the river, there were a few older men, with lines in the water, fishing. As Finn wondered how successful this primitive method might be, one of the men pulled the line towards himself out of the water, and on the end of it was a flailing fish. Finn murmured her admiration and the man who had caught the fish grinned, teeth flashing white in a scraggly red beard. Then he seemed to recognise her, and narrowed his eyes.

"I heard you were back," he said to Finn.

"Lothar," said Toby, quietly. "Serena has been talking about this for weeks. You knew they were coming. We don't need confrontation, we need unity."

"Just because she's been saying it for weeks doesn't mean we have to agree with it," spat Lothar. "It was her parents who got us into this mess in the first place. Finally, we get to the point where we're surviving, and doing OK. And you decide we need to attack now? It's crazy and it'll be the end of us."

"We don't have a choice," Toby said, still calm. "You know this. We've been through it together. PlanetRescue has taken over all the other communities, and we're going to be next."

"You've got no proof!" Lothar threw his line and fish on the ground. He walked over to stand too closely in front of Toby.

"You might have decided it was the best cause of action, but that doesn't mean the rest of us have been convinced. As far as I'm concerned, you're all insane. You're all celebrating the arrival of these two – " he gestured at Finn and Jhara "– but you're going to be sorry when it all goes to hell. And I promise I'll be the first to say I told you so!"

He glared at Finn and Jhara, and began to stride away from the river. The other two men looked uncomfortable, but they didn't say anything.

"Lothar is a little upset," Toby said, but didn't offer any other explanation.

Finn and Jhara looked at one another. Jhara furrowed her brow but Finn simply shrugged. Toby avoided eye contact and mumbled something about heading back.

"Might be a good idea," agreed Jhara. "I could do with a bit of a rest."

Finn shot her a look of concern, but Jhara waved a hand weakly.

"I'm OK. But I think I'd better not overdo it. Eleanor warned me that the medication might make it seem like I can do anything, and then I'd hurt myself even more."

Toby seemed happy that they were changing the subject, and began to talk to Jhara about the medication. He had some interest in learning about healing, he said, and Finn began to tune them out, walking a few steps behind them. She turned back to the two fishermen who were left on the riverbank and saw that they were looking back at her, too. They hadn't said anything when Lothar had yelled at Finn and Toby, so she wondered if that was because they didn't agree with him, or whether he was simply a mouthpiece for them. They broke their gaze first, and Finn turned around, and walked faster to catch up with Jhara and Toby.

They were talking about life in the City. Toby had many questions, and Jhara seemed happy to answer them. Their conversation lulled in the background while Finn mused over what Lothar had said, and how the small community would mobilise to attack the City.

They had reached the junction already and Jhara and Toby were waiting for her. They squinted back at her as she walked slowly to catch up. The sun was high in the sky, and the air was still. Finn was hot, and wished she were back inside.

"I was just saying it might be better if Jhara goes back to Eleanor's to rest," Toby suggested, looking from Finn back to Jhara. "It's where we keep all the medicine, plus of course, Eleanor's the one with the most experience."

Finn had hoped that Jhara might be able to come back to Serena and Toby's house, but Toby's plan seemed like a good one. She tried not to show her disappointment.

"I'll be fine," Jhara said. She smiled thinly.

They walked across the road with Jhara, who was much slower on her crutches than she had been before, when they'd set out. Toby went through the gate first to make sure the puppies were out of the way. He disappeared into the house and Finn touched Jhara's arm.

"Will you be all right there?" she asked. "You can ask to come back to Serena's, if you like."

Jhara shook her head.

"Eleanor is kind, and she knows what she's doing. I need the help. I'm going to need a lot of help. Sorry, Finn. I wish I'd never fallen. It was such a stupid mistake."

It was, but Finn knew Jhara would be upset if she said so.

"It doesn't matter," she replied. "Nothing we can do about it. Just hope that you get better soon, right?"

Toby called out to them from the doorway, and Finn opened the gate so that Jhara could make her way through, nervously choosing where she put her crutches so they wouldn't skid on the gravel path. She took her time getting up the steps to the house, and Finn could almost feel her exhaustion. As she reached doorway, Toby stepped aside and Eleanor appeared, her forehead creased with concern.

"Was it a bit too much for you then?"

"Oh, I'm fine," Jhara replied, but even Finn could hear the lie in her voice.

"Let's get you laid down then," said Eleanor, and walked

in front of Jhara as they headed into the cool darkness of the house.

Toby walked slowly down the steps towards Finn.

"Don't worry. She's safe with Eleanor."

Finn nodded, still watching Jhara's retreating back. Her head was beginning to throb from the midday brightness and a morning of interaction with strangers. Toby seemed to notice.

"Let's go home," he suggested. "You can have a rest if you need to. Nobody will mind if you're not up and about the whole time. We always planned for you to have a day of rest before we got stuck into the work. We need you to be at your best, you know."

Finn felt her head tighten further – she wasn't used to resting during the day, but this wasn't a normal day. Toby was quiet on the way back to Serena's house, leaving Finn with her thoughts. Once inside, she went straight to her room, and closed the door gently behind her.

The curtains blocked out most of the sunshine, except for a sliver of light at the edges. On her bed, a line of brightness cut across Finn's stomach, but her face was in darkness, and she closed her eyes and took deep breaths of the cool inside air. As she had done the night before, she searched her memories for any recollection of Seven Rivers. She wanted to prove to herself that she had lived here, but nothing surfaced. Everything she thought of was simply her mind, fabricating what she thought it might have been like. She didn't even have a memory of her parents, no idea of what they looked like. If only she had access to the World, she might be able to look for images of them. If PlanetRescue hadn't censored them, of course.

Coming to Seven Rivers meant making a connection with the past that Finn hadn't ever needed to make before. She wished Jhara were there in the room. Or Braithe. The unfamiliarity of everything drained her energy, along with the heat and that morning's confrontation at the river. Finn drew her knees to her chest and tucked her feet under the blanket, stretched her legs out, and drifted into sleep.

When she woke, it was with the disorienting sense that many hours had passed. Finn rubbed her hands over her face and stretched her limbs. The sleep had done her good but she felt hungry. She walked over the window and pulled back the curtains. The sun was low in the sky, and from her vantage point, she could see people enjoying the cool of the day, talking, tending to their gardens.

Finn let the curtain fall and listened for voices in the rest of the house. It sounded quiet, so she went to freshen up in the bathroom before walking through to the kitchen. Serena sat at the table, writing something. Finn noticed Toby's shoes weren't at the door. He must have gone out again.

"Sleep well?" asked Serena. "I checked on you and you were completely out of it. It's a lot to get used to, isn't it?"

Finn nodded.

"Would you like something to eat? I have leftovers here..."

Without waiting for an answer, she got up and opened the cupboard next to the fire, and took out a plate piled with food. Finn recognised potatoes and green beans, and there was some other mixture in a stew with a brown sauce. It smelled dark and salty. Finn felt her mouth water.

"A recipe from one of our neighbours," said Serena, as she set it down in front of Finn. "Would you like me to heat it in the pan for you?"

Finn shook her head. The plate still felt warm to the touch, and she gratefully accepted a spoon from Serena. It was like the others she'd used in Seven Rivers. Decades old, but it had been cared for. She rubbed her finger along the handle, thinking about how many others might have held it over the years. Maybe even people she'd known as a young child. Maybe even her family.

"Everything OK?"

Finn made brief eye contact with Serena and smiled.

"Yes. Thank you for the lunch."

Serena returned the smile and sat down opposite her again, picking up her pencil. They sat in silence for a few minutes while Finn ate and Serena wrote.

"Would you be able to..." Finn paused and pushed some of the potato around in the sauce. "Would you be able to tell me about what it was like out here? Before?"

Serena put her pen down and sat back in her chair. Finn wondered if she had annoyed her by interrupting her work, but Serena didn't look angry. Instead, she looked as if she were thinking about where to start.

"Well, we came out here in the '30s, Toby and I, as I told you last night. I'd heard that it was quieter over here in the west. So we crossed the Nullarbor and after floating around, camping here and there, we finally found out about Seven Rivers. We made our way over and they welcomed us here."

"How big… was it a lot different from how it is now?" Finn mixed the last of the vegetables together with the sauce and ate it all in one mouthful while she waited for Serena to reply.

"They didn't build it from nothing. There were a lot of abandoned towns. It was easier to start over in a place that already had some buildings, roads, tanks, that kind of thing. Seven Rivers was one of the more successful ones, because of the reliable water. But there were others. Some of the Elders – some of the ones you met – were already here. They were the ones who helped get it all going. I suppose when we got here, there would have been about thirty of us. Now there's about a hundred and fifty."

There was another short silence. Finn tried to imagine Seven Rivers, over two decades before, and the desperation which would have led people to escape to it.

"I've learned about the Collapse, obviously," she said. "But you lived through it. Toby, too, when he was really little. Was it that awful?"

Serena sighed.

"It's hard to be able to explain it. I suppose the images and collected thoughts you've seen inWorld would give you some idea, but the thing about it is that it didn't happen overnight. It was bad and then got worse, over months and years. So we knew it was happening, we thought it would just get better. Not just the environmental stuff, all the political issues and the refugees and people dying from heat waves and other unpredictable weather events. Honestly, I think most people just put their heads down and tried not to think about it. If I'd've been more aware, I'd have seen the writing was on the wall back then. It just took a threat to something – or someone – close to me to make me see how unsafe everything was getting."

Finn nodded.

"Not enough people were personally threatened, then," she said.

"That's pretty much it," agreed Serena. "I suppose history repeats itself like that. Look at the City now. If you keep your head down, you've several years of decent life there. You work hard, you have shelter and food. Why rock the boat? It's only once you get too old that you have to worry. Most Cityzens don't even think that far. They would rather not think about it all, really."

"But then you left, and found Seven Rivers," Finn said. "And things must have been OK, for a while."

"They were." Serena nodded. "It wasn't easy. People fought and argued, and we struggled with food and being able to work to each other's strengths. People died, even. Sometimes you can't help that. I remember..."

She stopped and blinked several times. Finn wondered if she were going to cry, but Serena smiled at her instead, even if the smile didn't seem that sincere.

"Some of the deaths were hard to take," she finished. "And most of us hadn't seen a dead body in our lives, or at least, not someone we knew. So that was difficult."

Serena sighed heavily.

"And you know, once we managed to find a way to negotiate with PlanetRescue, it was like there was... a compromise?"

She sounded wistful, Finn thought, and Serena seemed to realise it.

"I know, we were naïve. That's obvious to us now."

"So why did you decide to try and overthrow them, you and my parents and everyone?"

"You mean, why attack them when everything was going so well, right?"

Finn nodded.

"We thought that there would be some kind of certainty once everything had settled. After the Cities were built, I mean. Once we'd sorted out who would be in there and who would be staying out here… don't get me wrong, it's not like all of us chose to be outside the City. But most of us accepted it, and those who didn't could apply to be let in. That's how you ended up getting in, later, with Jhara and Braithe. But at first we figured that once people knew where they were, it would be stable, and it was for a while. Then we heard rumours. Not only about settlements like ours getting attacked, but also that entire Cities were being shut down."

Finn frowned.

"Why would they do that?"

Serena shrugged.

"We never found out. We tried, but there was no information coming out. PlanetRescue wouldn't say anything. And once a place is gone, then it's gone. Nobody left to tell the story, is there? So we didn't think it could be for any good reason. And that's why we decided to attack them."

"But that failed," Finn said, flatly.

"Yes, it did. We were foolish. Many people died. It took a long time to build up our resources again. PlanetRescue didn't trust us after that, of course. It was just us and the other communities. But then a few months ago, they started coming after them, too. Other settlements, we'd hear of them just being rounded up overnight. Or destroyed. Without warning."

"But what could they want from you?"

"The food… the fertiliser. The labour. It has to come from somewhere."

Braithe had told her about this, and Finn had even found some documents deep inWorld, but still, the horror of slavery and genocide suddenly made the air seem heavier.

Finn pushed her plate to one side.

"You said, yesterday, that this Revolution would be different because I was here. Why is that going to make any difference? What can I do?"

Serena looked at Finn with an intensity that made Finn uncomfortable.

"Braithe has been with you since you went to the City. She knows you, and she knows how you think. You're the smartest in your department at WorldSec. And you think outside the box."

"The box? What box?"

"I mean," Serena smiled, "we need you to come up with a solution. We need to be able to mobilise the Resistance in other Cities and communities. Up until now we've relied on travellers to send and receive messages. But we need to get the information out fast, and without PlanetRescue knowing. You're the only one who has the ability to crack the defences."

Serena sighed.

"I don't know how this will all play out," she said, looking down at the pencil, her fingers fidgeting with the end of it, where the wood was flaking away. "I suppose it just means something that you were able to get out of the City and get out here. It's the first time in twenty years. Nobody else has managed."

She looked up and smiled brightly at Finn, and closed the book she had been writing in. Finn got the impression that the conversation was over. She wondered if she had asked something awkward or inappropriate, but Serena didn't seem offended.

"Would you like to read something?" Serena said. She walked over to the drawers in the kitchen cabinet on the other side of the fire, and opened the top one. In it, Finn saw there were several thick books, like the one Serena had been writing in.

"These are our records," said Serena. "Before the Collapse, I'm talking way, way before, people used to record all this stuff in books like this. For all sorts of reasons, sometimes it was to remember what we had done or said, sometimes it was to remember an event. Computers came along and we started using them more, instead of writing it in books. But after the Collapse, when PlanetRescue controlled the computerised records, we realised we'd lost everything. So we started writing it down again, like before."

She picked up the stack and placed them heavily on the table.

"This will give you… some backstory. And there are also some stories of your parents in there, as well."

Finn raised her eyebrows.

"I don't know a lot about their past, but this gives you a place to start. And I need to be elsewhere for a few hours. Preparations. You know."

Finn nodded and reached for the first book. The cover was thick, and textured with lines criss-crossing the dark green. Finn rubbed her fingers on it, then picked it up carefully and placed it in front of her. It smelled strange, prompting an almost-memory which she couldn't place. She frowned, trying to hold onto it, but it was too elusive. Breathing in again, she eventually gave up and opened the book to the first, yellowed cover page.

Seven Rivers. 2036.

The year before I was born, thought Finn.

The entries were dated by seasons, not months. Finn smoothed the pages flat and began to read.

Warm start to the summer. We have planted seeds harvested from the more successful crops last season. Tomatoes growing under shade cloth, managed to trade some basil seed with farmers from Sheoak Grove. Gave them a young apple tree in return.

We have two pregnant women in the settlement at present. This news always brings a mixture of happiness and worry. Every few years we lose either the mother or the baby in childbirth, and even though Eleanor is experienced and does her best, sometimes things get complicated. We are all hoping that the babies will be born healthy and at full term.

Serena and Lothar have been negotiating with Western City. We think we're going to reach an agreement soon to swap access for fresh produce and meat. The access to the World will help us with communications between settlements and give us information about weather patterns and such, better than we have now, which is just making predictions based on observations and previous years' readings. With the weather being so changeable from year to year, we really need more reliable info.

Finn heard her name being called and looked up. Serena smiled.

"You're deep in that, huh? I called you a few times!"

Finn blushed.

"Sorry. I was… it's interesting."

"It really is. Feel free to read as much as you want. I have to go out, as I said. You're welcome to go and visit Jhara, too, if you'd like. Toby will be back later to cook. I'll see you tonight. OK?"

Finn nodded, and Serena held up her hand in farewell, then slipped on her shoes and left out the kitchen door. Even as she closed it behind her, Finn was absorbed again in the book.

Summer… negotiations are going well with

PlanetRescue. Lothar has misgivings about them coming to help us here in Seven Rivers, but Serena is convinced that we need to extend trust.

Late summer… we've just had a huge amount of rain and it's damaged many crops. The wheat is mouldy, we've lost apricots and grapes. Many of the herbs are a wet, slimy mess. It's upsetting to Eleanor, who uses them in her medicines. It's a blow to the rest of us, too. We've had to go further afield to trade, which puts more strain on the truck. Piet does what he can to fix it, but we've had to also trade for parts as well as food. Morale is low.

Early autumn… we had the PlanetRescue tech out for two days to help us with access. It was helpful. Lothar and three others went fishing up river for the duration. Lothar wants the service but believed we could have managed to do it ourselves with instructions, rather than having Cityzens come to the Badlands. The tech doesn't speak to us, even though he does smile and seems friendly. Who knows what he's been told about us?

Mid-autumn… we lost one of the babies last night. Eleanor still not sure why, but it was too little and couldn't be saved. Everyone very quiet and sad this morning.

Finn looked up, her heart beating hard. It was that easy, that a baby could die. She could have died. She pushed the book away from her, keeping her finger on the entry. The other baby would have been about her age, which meant that the other pregnant woman might have been her mother. This was why Serena had given her the books to read. This was Finn's beginning. She lowered her eyes to the page again.

Early winter… it's been cold, frost on the gardens and the sides of the valleys in the mornings. We've been doubling up, older folk moving into family houses with younger ones, so we can reduce the fuel use and use our body heat to keep the rooms warm. It's working, although we've still got two infants and one of the Elders sick with pneumonia. Eleanor is doing all she can.

We had some travellers come through – a man and a woman on their way over to the east. They stayed three days. Interesting couple – he was a mechanic before the Collapse and she was a chemist. A few of us stayed up talking to them, late in the evenings. It's always good to hear what news travellers bring. They'd been past Western City but weren't interested in staying, even though their skills would have been in demand. When we asked why, the woman just tugged at her grey hair and smiled, and said she thought she'd be past the use-by date. Not sure if this is confirmation of the stories that the Cities euthanise their elderly or sick, or just more of the same rumours.

The man tinkered with our truck and looked at a couple of the batteries which hadn't been charging well. The woman talked to us a bit about medicines. Her specialty wasn't pharmaceuticals but she had some useful tips all the same. She told us over tea about how she'd worked on a government investigation into the sulphur dioxide cocktail PlanetRescue had used which caused the flooding and the fallout. "Of course it was shut down before we could pursue it properly," she said, in a resigned sort of way. We nodded. Of course it was. We all knew how the governments fell into line behind PlanetRescue.

Spring… We keep hearing word of the new governor of Western City. Her name is Eva and she's regional governor of the whole of the East Sector. 411 Cities in total. She's supposedly ruthless, really toes the line for PlanetRescue. They're cracking down on refugees, there is talk of Cities being completely shut off and left on their own. We can only imagine how they're faring. Hopefully some of the communities on the outside are helping them out. All those Cityzens... they'll have forgotten how to do anything for themselves. If they even knew how to do anything to begin with.

Finn felt her irritation curdle inside. The writer had made it sound as if Cityzens were completely incapable. So typical. She huffed to herself and thought about her daily life in the City: woken by the central computer, before she collected her breakfast ration which was delivered in the early morning by a staff roster. Then dressing in freshly laundered PlanetRescue regulation clothing, before catching an autodriver to work.

Finn smiled ruefully. The writer was right. Most Cityzens really couldn't look after themselves, Finn included. She rubbed her eyes. It was getting dark outside; she could see the shadows lengthening out the kitchen window. She stood up, still feeling the stretch in her legs from the walk the day before. It would be good to move around before nightfall. She slipped on her shoes and opened the kitchen door.

Outside, it was quieter than before. Work was winding down for the day with the waning sunlight, and Finn noted that most people seemed relaxed as they talked with each other, collecting in threes and fours on the dirt road, in front of their houses, sitting on steps. They seemed to inhabit each other's spaces, sharing the communal areas but also their own houses. The City had strict rules about how much time the Cityzens were to spend with one another. Finn frowned as she thought about it. It hadn't been something which bothered her, content as she was in her own company. But it had bothered Braithe, enough for her to mention it to Finn and Jhara about how unhealthy it was.

"People can't even sleep together, can't be together," she would mutter. "It's not how humans are supposed to be. We're supposed to make connections. Community. That's what humans are about!"

Jhara would roll her eyes and remind her mother that sex was allowed, but most Cityzens never bothered.

"It's not like they even care, Mama," she said. "It's not like decades ago, when it was frowned upon if you weren't married. They don't care who you sleep with, how many, boy or girl. It's a drive, like hunger. And why bother, when nobody's hungry?"

"It's not like hunger," Braithe would mutter. "It's about more than sex, Jhara. Although how I expect you to understand something you've never experienced, I don't know…"

Finn had never paid much attention to these conversations. She had been interested in her work, not any of her colleagues. There were employees in her division at WorldSec who would go to the block's private rooms for sex, she knew that. But there was no sleeping all night together, in shared accommodation, not like here.

Walking down the steps, she wove her way quietly between them. Most people nodded or acknowledged her as she went through. Word obviously travelled quickly – they all knew who she was, but nobody stopped her, and Finn was soon at Eleanor's house, as the grey of evening began to filter out the light.

She opened the garden gate slowly, prepared for the dogs she had met earlier, but they were absent. Finn felt anxiety churning in her stomach. Serena had said it would be fine to visit Jhara, but Finn still felt nervous at arriving at a stranger's door without having someone familiar with her. She talked herself into a timid knock, and then decided she would go if nobody answered. Just as she was deciding how long to wait, the door opened, and Eleanor stood there, with a kind expression, as if Finn were exactly the person she were expecting.

"Jhara is still sleeping," Eleanor said.

"Oh, I'll come back later, then," Finn said hurriedly, and turned to leave, but Eleanor put her hand out towards her.

"Not at all! Come on in. I have something to show you."

Finn hesitated, but wasn't sure of the right way to refuse, so instead, nodded and stepped over the threshold.

Eleanor led her into the kitchen, where some kind of stew was simmering on the top of the wood-burning stove. Eleanor stirred it once or twice, and turned to Finn.

"I just wanted to check to make sure it wasn't catching on the bottom of the pot," she said. "Come on, out the back. It's dark enough."

Finn was curious, but said nothing. She followed Eleanor down the passageway, past the room where Jhara was staying. The door was ajar and she could see Jhara's sleeping form. It reassured her.

"Here," said Eleanor in a soft voice. "Come out into the back garden. Don't worry, Ian's taken the dogs to stay with some friends. It's just us. I needed it to be dark because I wanted to show you the sky."

Finn stepped down onto the gravel and looked up. Eleanor was pointing.

"This sky… I think we always imagined, back before the Collapse, that we would find ourselves somewhere up there, too. Escaping to the stars. But here we are, still on Earth. Oh, well."

She glanced over at Finn, and gave her hand a quick squeeze.

"Your mother was an expert on navigating by the stars."

Finn searched Eleanor's face in the darkness.

"You were friends with my mother?"

"Yes, good friends. I got to know her when she was pregnant with you. And then of course, I delivered you, and she used to bring you around when you were a baby. We would drink tea and talk while you played on the kitchen floor. She left you with me the night she and your father died."

Eleanor's voice cracked.

"After the Collapse, death was so close, all the time. I know you are sheltered from it in the City. It's not something you ever deal with, and that was the way for many of us before the Collapse. Even working in hospitals, we had so much to rely on, different drugs, computers..."

She sighed.

"The Collapse changed all that. In some ways, it was an equaliser. Before, we were so privileged in the major cities, and in more developed countries. So once all our technology was too expensive for most of us, we had to rely on other knowledge. That's why it was so good to come together in these communities."

Eleanor put her hand on Finn's arm and smiled.

"Your mother was a kind woman. I know you've probably heard some things about her, and you might have wondered why she would leave you, but I want you to know that she believed very strongly that they would win against PlanetRescue that night. They would never have gone, if they thought they wouldn't come back."

Finn knew that Eleanor expected her to say something, but before she could think of anything, the moment passed. Eleanor was looking up at the sky again, and pointing out the brightest stars.

"At least we can see them more clearly, now," she said. "Whatever we miss from the days before the Collapse, we had trouble seeing the stars. Too much light and smog. Pollution. But now... the way the forests have regenerated. The wildlife. There is a kind of peace, I suppose."

Her voice trailed off as she sighed. She seemed contented, Finn thought, like so many of them here. No wonder some of them didn't want to fight PlanetRescue. They just wanted to stay here and live their lives. They had settled and didn't want to leave. Especially if it meant that it might change everything forever. Some of them must have had more than enough change in their lifetimes.

She sat on the step, and Eleanor turned, and smiled, and sat near her. They didn't speak, and Finn felt comfortable in the silence.

Eleanor leaned forward to stand, and Finn realised that she might be the best person to ask about her history.

"Tell me about them?" she said suddenly into the darkness.

Eleanor seemed surprised, but she leant back again and looked up to the sky.

"Oh," she murmured, "where to start...?"

Finn waited, wordless.

"Your mother was already pregnant with you when they arrived. They came from the east – so, through the desert, we assumed. But it was common back then... or even now, I suppose, not to talk about your history. So they didn't say, and we didn't ask. I don't know anything about their time before they came to Seven Rivers. I'm sorry I can't tell you about that."

Finn swallowed.

"But the City was so strict..."

"You mean, why did PlanetRescue accept you, given that they'd locked down the City? That's a bit more complicated. You might have heard that only the elite could get in – that they kept out anyone who couldn't work. Well, I think someone probably took pity on you all. And maybe there was some hope that Braithe would offer intel. I don't know. As for inside the Cities, there was an imbalance. For sure. But that existed in society. It's been that way for centuries. I meant what I said about the Collapse being an equaliser but the structure reaffirmed itself. Those who'd been in power before found power again."

"So it doesn't matter who my parents were? Where I came from?"

"Of course it matters!" Eleanor's eyes crinkled as she smiled at Finn, and she squeezed her hand again. "It matters because it's *you*. That's what makes me so sad that I can't help you find out more about it. But I'm sorry, I don't know."

She pressed her hands together and crossed one thumb over the other.

"So many of us lost our history after the Collapse. There were rumours that PlanetRescue were hunting out people from different backgrounds. I don't know whether it was true or if it was just rumours. If it helps, you're not alone. We've all had to find another community, patch together stories about their past. Where we land, we blend together what we remember, and we add in what is useful. I suppose that's the way culture has developed over time. It doesn't make it right, of course. And we've lost a lot of history that way. But it is what it is."

She looked over at Finn, who was listening, focusing on the stones in the garden which were barely visible in the darkness.

"I've given you a lot to think about, I imagine."

Finn nodded, and Eleanor stood up.

"You can stay out here for a while, if you like. I know Serena will be expecting you back later, but there's no rush. Jhara may wake up, and you can talk to her, or you can just sit and look at the stars. Let me know if you need anything."

She walked back up the stairs, and Finn was left alone in the dark garden, as the last of the light faded along the horizon in the west.

Jhara stayed asleep until the stars were bright in the sky and the town had quietened down into murmurs behind closed doors, and Eleanor suggested that Finn come back in the morning to see her.

"You need your rest, too," she said. "The work starts in earnest tomorrow."

Finn reluctantly walked back towards Serena's house. The soft light from the windows of the houses fell onto the dirt and now and then, she saw people moving around. She wondered whether her parents had spent their evenings in the same way: talking with friends, or each other. Eating together. People coming and going between their small houses. By the time she got to Serena's front door, Finn ached with a longing for that life.

She struggled through the evening, making as much small talk as she could manage, and then excused herself when they had eaten.

"Of course," Serena said when she mentioned that she wanted to turn in for the night. "Rest. Sleep well."

Finn smiled briefly, and headed back to her room, shut the door, and leant against it. Things had been so clear when she had left the City with Jhara, and the idea of what they were going to do seemed so logical. Now, being here in the community, with a history – her own history – constantly coming up in conversation, and confrontation of the plan and all that she and Jhara had set in motion, it didn't seem so simple anymore.

Without even bothering to undress, Finn climbed into the unmade bed, and despite her hours-long nap earlier in the day, she fell asleep within minutes.

Chapter 5

After breakfast the next day, Finn walked back along the dirt road, the soft sand and occasional small stone now feeling familiar under her feet. Jhara was sitting at the kitchen table with Eleanor. She looked less pale than she had the day before, and smiled more easily.

Eleanor put a mug of tea down in front of Finn without asking, and Finn made what she hoped was a grateful expression.

"I've got gardening to do over at the community plot," Eleanor said as she put her own empty cup in the sink. "Plenty of food in the cupboard. Don't go hungry while I'm gone!"

She grabbed a hat off a hook near the kitchen door and waved as she walked out.

"Do you think she just wanted to give us a chance to talk?" Jhara asked, leaning back in her chair and adjusting her injured leg.

"I came over last night to see you."

"I know. Eleanor told me."

"Well, I spoke to her about living here... about my

parents, and what it was like before the Collapse."

Finn paused.

"I guess it's just hard to accept that there was... another life. I can't believe I don't remember anything."

"Finn, you were a baby."

"I know. But I feel... missing."

"Like you missed out?"

"No. Like I'm missing."

Jhara frowned.

"I mean... as if I don't have a place where I belong." Finn folded her arms across her body. "That I'm missing, and I don't know where home is. So many of the comments have been about me coming back, and it's like I have their history here, but it's not mine."

She sighed.

"It's all supposed to be normal and familiar and it's not. They have lives and we're just..."

Jhara smiled, and reached across the table, but they both knew she wouldn't touch Finn when she was in this mood.

"Everything is different," Finn continued. "I like it but it's different. I want to belong but then I don't. There is no World and the food is different and it's hot and cold and… outside."

Jhara snorted a laugh.

"You don't like it because it's outside?"

"You know what I mean. And there is no World."

"You said that."

Finn shrugged. Jhara folded her fingers together around her mug of tea.

"You knew it would be different," she said. "Braithe explained everything."

"I know she did. But there… I couldn't understand it until I was in it."

Jhara nodded and Finn sat back in her chair. They sat in silence for a moment and Finn's eyes were drawn to the ceiling, and its symmetrical pattern, embossed onto the surface.

"It's pressed tin, Eleanor says," Jhara told her.

"That's what I mean! That there! There's no point to it. I know that PlanetRescue has done awful things. But the City… at least everything had a reason. There was nothing unnecessary. It all had purpose."

Jhara laughed out loud.

"It's art, Finn!"

"Well, I don't like it."

"Help me up," Jhara said, pushing her chair back as best she could. "You sound bad-tempered. Maybe more outside is just what you need – sorry. I'm kidding. But you could do with some distraction. Talking about how much you hate everything isn't going to make you feel better."

Finn frowned but didn't have a good argument against Jhara, so did as she asked. She had managed to help Jhara to stand when there was a call down the hallway, and Toby appeared at the kitchen door.

"Oh, good. You're up," Toby said. "I need to show you the communications hut. We're going to have to get started on contacting the Resistance today, if we can. If *you* can."

They took a different path towards the water, which led behind Eleanor's house and back up the road where they had come in two days before. Finn looked along the road and wondered about Braithe and the rest of the Cityzens. Jhara followed her gaze and nodded.

"Over here is where we used to swim when we were younger," Toby said, interrupting them and pointing out a small hill. "The kids still play there, and it's not too steep a walk. There's a seat there for you, too, Jhara."

Finn took another look at her friend, who looked tired already, but Jhara just nodded and set off along the path behind Toby. As Finn followed them both, she looked over at the other side of the river, where the land stretched into the distance, scrubby trees a line across the horizon. The hills were aged and gentle. No sheer cliffs or spiked mountaintops. The vastness of it made her feel strange – alone and insignificant, but also very free. She felt like she could stretch and shout and nobody would care. This place was one of otherness, and the people would simply shrug and smile. She wondered how she had accepted the conformity of the City for so long.

Up ahead, Toby and Jhara were already sitting on a long wooden bench. Finn realised that her own legs were beginning to ache, and welcomed the chance to rest. As Toby had said, there were some children playing in the mud at the edge of the river, and splashing in the shallows. Now that the sun was above them, Finn was beginning to feel warm, and sweat prickled the back of her neck and under her arms. Having experienced the bath two days before, she expected that the cool water splashing on legs and arms would feel just as good, and she envied the children.

"Are you feeling all right?" Jhara asked her gently.

"I'm OK," Finn smiled. "Tired from the walk, still."

"I know what you mean," Jhara agreed, holding her crutches to one side, and leaning her head against them. "Me, too."

"You didn't do anything!" grinned Finn. "Spent all day and night lying down..."

Jhara picked up a crutch and threatened to hit Finn with it. Finn laughed, ducked, and stood up from the bench, stepping back a few steps and bumping into Serena, who gave a little shriek of surprise. Finn blushed.

"Toby said you'd be out here. You'll be able to see our communications, Finn. Hopefully it'll be something you can work with," said Serena, holding out an arm, in case Finn lost her balance. "How are you feeling today, Jhara?"

Jhara nodded.

"Better. Thank you."

Serena held up a hand and squinted against the sun, looking upriver.

"I have some people to see this morning," she said. "But things are hopefully moving. I'd like to talk to you all about what to expect over the next day or so. I was hoping we could all sit down at lunch together."

They nodded.

"Good. I'll see you all at lunchtime, then!"

Serena smiled and headed back off towards some of the other houses, through waist high bushes. Small birds darted from the air and caught flying insects in their beaks as Serena disturbed the leaves. Finn caught a waft of a new scent on the wind, and asked Toby about it.

"It's lavender and rosemary," he said. "When Serena walked through here, the leaves brushed past her, and it released the oils. We plant them down here because we don't water this area, and they stand up to the dry. And the bees love them, too."

Finn walked over and took a leaf from one of the plants, and held it to her nose.

"Squash it between your fingers."

"Huh," said Finn, "it's so… sharp."

Toby laughed.

"Well, that's one way to put it. It's supposed to be calming, too. Feel calmer?"

Finn shrugged, and he grinned again.

"Maybe it doesn't work on Cityzens… I'm kidding!"

Jhara had given him a dig in the ribs.

"Fair enough. I'm sorry. Let's get to the hut. See if we can get in touch with the City."

Finn felt a jab of excitement at the chance to once again experience the familiar.

Toby pointed to a building not far from where they were sitting. They followed a narrow path through the low bushes, as Serena had done. Where she had gone to the closest house, however, Finn, Jhara and Toby veered off the west and headed towards a smaller hut, which stood on its own. On the roof was a tall aerial, and the same solar panels as on other houses, but this building had more of them. There were also fewer windows – just one at the front, near the door.

"The aerial is to boost radio signal," Toby explained as they reached the steps up to the front door.

"Radio...?" Finn was confused. "You said this was how you got inWorld."

"Well, we can get inWorld, via old phone lines. Or we used to be able to. The Resistance rigged them up... it's old tech and it worked for a bit. Now, the connection fails, more often than not. I guess PlanetRescue is reluctant to have

Badlanders accessing the information they think they own."

He stopped and grinned at Finn again.

"You'd have firsthand experience of that, though."

Finn felt her cheeks grow hot again. She wondered if she had ever blocked Toby or the others from Seven Rivers, trying to get inWorld. She felt a pang of guilt.

"I'm kidding," Toby said. "Really. Nobody is upset at you for that."

He opened the door and held it open for them. Jhara struggled up the steps and Finn walked slowly behind her.

Inside, it was cool and dark. Toby shut the door and pulled a lever on the wall next to the doorframe. On the ceiling, some shutters slid back to reveal skylights, and filtered sunlight spread across the large room.

Finn had expected some old-style computer, probably from the 2020s, but instead, there was a built-in desk, all the way around the walls, with wooden stools similar to those in Serena's house. Two black rectangular boxes sat on the desks, each with a battery pack taped to them. Someone had made a switch and written numbers on the outside of the boxes. Finn narrowed her eyes, straining to read them, but she couldn't make sense of it. There was a cord from each leading up to a small hole in the roof, and each had a set of headphones and a microphone on a stand in front of them.

"This is our communications centre," said Toby, watching Finn and Jhara as they both looked around. "You're impressed, I can tell."

Finn nodded, not wanting to hurt his feelings. Jhara chuckled, and Finn realised she'd missed another joke. But these machines really did seem backward.

"How do they even work?" she said.

She walked over and picked up a set of headphones, and put them on, but heard nothing.

"Getting inWorld has been too difficult, so we gave up on the computers. What's more necessary is getting in touch with the Underground in the City. And we don't need computers for that. We can use radio."

"Radio..." echoed Finn quietly. "Of course!"

Toby walked over to the desk and pulled two stools out, and indicated for them to sit.

"So we realised at the beginning that just talking on the radio would be too dangerous," he said, flicking a couple of switches on the box so that several lights came on. "When Braithe and the others moved to the City, they installed radio sets at two places in the ventilation shafts. One in the east shaft and one in the north."

He turned a dial, and they heard static scratching inside the speaker.

"We knew PlanetRescue would be listening to the channels."

"They would," agreed Finn. "Even if you used code, they would probably be able to break it. There is a whole department within WorldSec, working on it."

"So we switched between the channels, changing it every day so they'd have trouble tracing it..."

He turned the dial more and the static grew louder, then hushed to a quiet prickle of sound. Toby took the microphone and pressed a button on the stand, in an uneven rhythm. Finn didn't notice anything, and wondered if she were missing something significant. He turned and smiled.

"Just wait," he said.

They sat and watched the radio. A half minute passed and Finn was about to ask what it was they were waiting for, when the static suddenly stopped for a moment, and then resumed, in a similar uneven rhythm.

Finn gasped quietly and looked at Toby, who smiled

again.

"It's..."

"Shh," he said, holding up a hand.

The breaks in the static continued at intervals, with irregular breaks. Toby was listening, concentrating. After a few moments the static resumed, unbroken, and Toby took the microphone again and clicked the button a few more times. When he had finished, he turned back to Finn, and raised his eyebrows.

"It's Morse," she said.

"Yes it is."

Finn rubbed her bottom lip with her thumb.

"I would never have thought of that," she admitted.

"Well, I don't think the rest of WorldSec has either. The simplest solution is usually the best. I remember some philosopher or something saying it. And it's true. Especially in this case."

He sat back on his stool and looked at both of them.

"Anyway. The Underground says all preparations are proceeding as planned. They're happy to hear you're recovering, Jhara. Braithe is very proud of you, and of Finn."

Jhara looked from the radio to Toby, and back again.

"OK. What am I missing?"

"The gaps… they're letters," explained Finn. "You know. Morse code."

"Like a secret language, then?" said Jhara.

"You don't know about Samuel Morse? Nineteenth century? Alfred Vail…"

Finn broke off as Jhara shook her head.

"Some of us actually read for pleasure, you know. In our time off," Jhara grinned. "Unlike some people, who spend all their time inWorld, studying codebreaking and secret languages."

"Yes, and look how that's working out for us now?" smiled Finn.

"OK, fair," Jhara shrugged. "So… the Underground. They're ready?"

"Almost. Normally we wouldn't have someone simply there to answer – we only communicate at prearranged times. It's too dangerous otherwise. The person on the other end has to go into the tunnel and they're exposed to patrols on the way in and out. But PlanetRescue is getting desperate, and they probably know that something is going on, so Braithe said she was going to try and have communications covered as many hours of the day as she could. PlanetRescue already knows you're both missing."

"When did they find out?" Finn asked. "We half-expected them to come after us when we were in the Dead Zone, but they didn't."

"According to the Underground, it took them until last night. Your little trick with the security worked better than expected. Kept them busy for a good while. So well done on that."

Finn blushed slightly and Jhara pushed her gently.

"See? Knew you'd be good for something eventually."

"Early this morning," Toby went on, "PlanetRescue cut off all access to the World for its Cityzens."

Finn and Jhara gasped.

"What? So nobody can get inWorld? Not even in the City?"

"They've blocked the signal somehow. One of our Underground says it's probably just a simple change to the connection."

"Likely just a change in server access," Finn said, "where they –"

"Yes, thank you for that, nerdling," interrupted Jhara.

"What I want to know is, how does this change the plan? Are they OK? Braithe?"

"She's fine," said Toby. "She's sent messages through to us. It just means none of them can use the World. That's obviously a disadvantage, but it's not disastrous. I mean, we manage OK, don't we?"

"But we need to get in contact with the other Cities, right?" Jhara said. "Doesn't that make it harder for Finn?"

"Well, yeah, there is that."

Finn was quiet for some moments, staring at the radio. The other waited for her to say something, and when she remained silent, Jhara nudged her.

"Nothing to say about this, then, WorldSec Engineer?"

Finn slowly shook her head, but she still said nothing.

Toby and Jhara exchanged glances.

"Well, we probably need to get back," Toby said. "Don't forget Serena wants to talk to us at lunch. She probably has some news from this morning."

Finn nodded, still quiet. She barely noticed the concern on Jhara's face as they walked through the low shrubs. Absently, she pulled at the leaves of the passing bushes, smelling again the herbs as she crushed them between her fingers.

When they got to the steps of Serena's house, Jhara put a crutch in front of her to stop her.

"What's going on with you?" she asked. "Do I need to worry?"

Finn shook her head.

"Just thinking," she said.

It was cooler inside, and Serena was readying the table for them.

"Leftovers for lunch, and what I've just grabbed out of the garden," she said. "Hope you don't mind."

"Get outta here with your false modesty," Toby laughed. "It'll be delicious, and you know it."

Serena gave him a slap on the back of the head, but Finn saw her smiling.

"The last of the tomatoes, and some lettuce leaves, and the bread from yesterday, plus some berries…"

"It looks just amazing," Jhara said.

They sat down around the wooden table. Finn was struck again by how strong the flavours were – sweet and acid and salty, almost to the point of overwhelming. Meals here seemed to take on an event status, a celebration worth time and concentration, instead of an allocated break from work or sleep.

"So you went to see the communications hut?" Serena asked. "What did you think?"

"Finn was impressed with your code," said Jhara. "She's hardly spoken since. I think she can't quite believe it."

Serena raised her eyebrows and looked over at Finn.

"Is that right?"

"No…" said Finn, slowly.

"It's not?" Serena seemed confused.

"It's not the Morse which…" Finn began, then paused, tapping the back of her fork against her cheek. "The World."

She looked around at the others.

"Finn," Jhara reminded her, "we are not in your head. You're going to have to explain what you're thinking."

Finn smiled and blushed.

"Sorry," she said. "I do that."

She paused.

"You said you wanted me to get inWorld."

Serena sighed, and put down the tomato she was about to eat.

"Yes. Without it, we have limited access to the Cityzens

but also we can't communicate with any other Cities, and if we go in without it, then our chances of success are lowered, because we are only in contact with the Underground in Western City. So there is a risk that PlanetRescue will be able to turn all the Cityzens against us. Plus bring in reinforcements from other Cities."

"You were hoping to release the real story behind the Cities... the way PlanetRescue has manipulated the information in the World," Finn said.

"Yes, we... something like that," replied Serena, looking to Toby and then back at Finn. "Have you... who discussed this with you?"

"Nobody," shrugged Finn. "It seemed like the natural progression. I just figured... and my guess is that PlanetRescue figured it out, too. And that's why they shut off the World. So you couldn't get in, and so that any information you did get in would be hard to spread. The Underground has to be careful who it trusts, doesn't it?"

"Unfortunately, yes," admitted Toby.

"I have an idea how you could get inWorld again."

Serena and Toby stopped eating. Jhara looked at them both and smiled a small smile.

"It's not like we haven't tried," Toby said. "We have – we've tried everything. We just get blocked."

"I know," said Finn, wryly. "I was one of the ones blocking you. Obviously that was before I knew you."

"Obviously," said Toby.

"But I think we can get inWorld without going through the City. We go straight to the source, and hack it from there."

"The source?" Serena asked. "What source?"

"The satellite," Finn said, pointing up to the ceiling. "We build our own satellite dish, and we'll have access to everything we need. I'll also be able to see the block they're using, which is preventing the Cityzens from getting inWorld."

"You're assuming that they haven't changed codes or that there won't be some kind of wall to keep you out," Jhara argued.

"I'd thought of that, and you're right. They probably expect us to try and get in, and they'll be trying to stop us. But I think I'll be able to get around that. I hope…"

She looked at Serena and Toby, and saw their concern and reluctance.

"We don't have anything to lose, right?"

Serena looked as if she were about to speak, but paused for a few minutes. Nobody said anything.

"No," she said, finally, although with some uncertainty. "We don't."

"I think what Serena is saying is that there could be some resistance," Toby offered.

Serena nodded. Finn remembered the reaction of the fishermen. She looked down at her plate and thought for a moment, then looked up to meet Serena's gaze.

"Isn't resistance what you do best, though?" Finn said, with a small smile.

Serena laughed and sighed.

"This is true."

"So we need materials to make a dish," said Finn.

"Probably be able to salvage something from the scrapyard, right?" Toby said, looking at Serena for confirmation.

"That would be a good place to start," agreed Serena. "Jhara can stay here with me, if it's easier?"

Jhara nodded.

"I'm not really looking forward to any more walking today. I might even lie down for a bit."

"Of course."

Serena got up to help Jhara out of her chair, and Finn noticed that her face seemed drawn and tired. The pain was obviously returning. They had done so much walking around during the morning. She had forgotten that Jhara's leg, although well set and cared for, would still be very sore.

"I'll be fine," Jhara said, noticing Finn's concern. "You go tinker about with the dish and I'll look forward to seeing a full demonstration when I get up."

She smiled at Finn, a taut, sad smile, and Finn felt a stab of pity for her. She imagined that if Braithe were there, Jhara would feel a lot better. For want of something wise or helpful to say, Finn simply smiled back, and watched Serena and Jhara make their way slowly through the doorway and down the short passage to the back of the house, where Finn had slept the night before.

"Serena knows injuries," said Toby. "Jhara is in good hands."

"I'm not worried," lied Finn. She avoided Toby's eyes. "You want to get started on this, then?"

"Yep. It would be ideal if we could get this done and try it out before nightfall. We don't have heaps of time. We'll take the bike and trailer, I think. It'll be easier to collect what we need."

He opened a drawer in the cabinet and pulled out a tool and some rope and a notebook and pencil.

"The bike is a bit dodgy," he acknowledged. "But it pays to be prepared for when something falls off… which it usually does. The notebook's for you, though. Write down what you think we need and then we can make sure we don't forget anything? Best to get it all in one trip if we can."

Finn raised her eyebrows and took the notebook. Toby laughed at her expression.

"I know, I'm amazingly well organised when I need to be. Mostly, I just don't want to be making another run over there in the dark to get the stuff we forgot."

His humour was infectious and Finn allowed herself a brief smile before sitting back at the table and starting on the list. She thought back to all the hours she had spent researching pre-Collapse communication technology, "nerding out" as Jhara used to call it. It had been one of her personal projects, and she felt a quiet pride at being able to finally use all this information that others had dismissed as boring and useless.

She could feel Toby looking at her, so she quickly checked over the list and nodded, then followed him outside. It was quiet, and she guessed that most people were still eating their midday meal. The afternoon was warm, and the air felt thick. Toby seemed uncomfortable, tugging on the front of his shirt to move air around his body.

"Getting a bit overcast," he said, looking up. "We might get some rain tonight." Then he grinned. "It'll have been a while since you experienced rain, won't it?"

Finn nodded slowly, studying the clouds. It was hard to equate the concept of gases building up in the atmosphere with these thick billows.

"Wait until sunset," Toby said. "The colours should be amazing."

He collected the bike and trailer from the side of the house. He was right, Finn thought, the bike seemed like it was about to fall apart, but the trailer seemed to be sturdy. It was made of wood, and attached with two long arms to a twisted wire at the back of the bike, under the seat. Finn was surprised it even held together, but she supposed it must work well enough. *The simplest solution was usually the best*, she remembered.

Toby pushed the bike and they walked down the road they had taken earlier, when they had gone to visit Jhara. Instead of turning at Eleanor's house, they continued onwards and then turned down another path. There were only a few houses there, and Finn noticed they'd come to the end of the settlement, where the cows and sheep were kept, and the larger gardens and crops were planted. Behind the crops were tall trees, some still in bloom, some already bearing fruit. In the understorey were vines; Finn squinted to see grapes sheltering under dark green leaves. Small lizards darted along fence posts and hid in the cracked wood. Past the rows of leafy stalks, she saw a fenced yard, with large piles of metal – old bits of cars and tractors, tyres, doors, windows, and all the pieces of machine which had been part of a life before the Collapse.

"We collected these from other communities," Toby explained. "Took several years, but most people didn't want them and were happy to give them to us. We have a couple of mechanics, so they welcomed the chance to tinker with them. That's how they got the truck going."

He pointed over to the right side of the road and Finn saw the truck Toby and Serena had travelled in, to collect her and Jhara from the Badlands.

"It's our only working vehicle, though," he said. "So obviously we only use it when we really have to. Trade, that sort of thing. I mean, when we used to trade."

"You don't anymore?" Finn asked. "Why not?"

Toby looked back at her, squinting into the sun.

"There's nobody left to trade with," he said, simply.

"There's… nobody?" Finn repeated.

She stopped walking, and stared at Toby as he turned back.

"We're the last ones," said Toby, continuing on to the yard where the fence stopped and there was an open gate. "Us and Bright Falls, about two hours east of here. I thought Braithe and Serena would have told you."

Finn shook her head.

"It's why we have to succeed," Toby said. "This is our last shot. PlanetRescue have managed to take over all the other communities, on this side of the desert, at least. We're the last, and we've been holding out, but now it's do or die."

He stopped and looked back, waiting for her to catch up.

"And when I say, 'die'…" he said, his eyes solemn.

"I understand," Finn said. "I know what they can do."

"We've lost too much," Toby continued. He left the bike and walked over to the closest heap of scrap metal and climbed up the side. "I know that some of the people here want to stay out of it, but I'm not willing to just let them continue to keep taking and taking. We're on a dying planet, anyway. We have to stop them from taking everything."

Finn nodded. Toby, already busily shifting vehicle parts out of the way, seemed unbothered whether she offered any solution.

"So what are we looking for?" Toby asked, standing with one foot on the edge of a car door and looking down at Finn.

Finn put a thumb to her lips and thought for a moment.

"We need a large disk..." she began. "The electronics... I think I will be able to rig from one of your radios. We'll need some kind of conduit..."

Toby began to scramble over the heap, tossing bits of historic trash to the side as he went. Finn searched close the ground, trying to will the materials to reveal themselves. The disorder of the heaps was extremely unsettling. After a few minutes, Toby called out to her, and she looked up, holding her palm above her eyes to block out the brightness.

"How's this?" He held up a large shiny flat object. "I think it came from a weather balloon. I remember finding it, years ago."

He turned it over in his hands.

"It's held up really well," he shrugged, and began to step, sure-footed, down the hillside of scrap towards Finn.

"What else do we need?" he asked, looking at the list.

Finn shifted her weight from foot to foot; the heat and humidity was giving her a headache. She wished they had just gathered everything already, and she could start putting it all together, somewhere darker and cooler.

"You OK?" Toby asked.

"Yes."

"No you're not. Is the heat getting to you?"

Finn shrugged.

"Listen, leave me here. I've got the list. You go back to the house and tell Serena to send some others to come and help me."

"By myself?"

"Well, yeah. You don't need me to walk you back, do you? You know the way."

"But the fishermen..." Finn began.

"They're more bluster than anything else. They probably

wouldn't even say anything if you were walking by yourself."

Finn felt the panic rising the way it had when she and Jhara were about to jump out of the tunnel into the Badlands. But Jhara wasn't there now, and she didn't want to melt down in front of Toby. She moved her tongue in her dry mouth and swallowed.

"OK. Serena will know who to get," she repeated quietly to herself.

"She will. Some mates of mine. I'd tell you their names but it's just something else to remember. You'll meet them later anyway."

He stood up and took a swig from the water bottle, then offered it to Finn.

"Thank you," she said, after several mouthfuls. "You'll be OK here on your own?"

"Yes, just as you'll be OK walking back to the house. Stop stalling and go."

He smiled, taking the cool glass bottle back from her.

"See you later on, then. Serena can probably help you with the conduit and cables you need, as well. We can dismantle one of the radios, if that's what it takes."

"Sure," Finn replied, holding up her hand in an awkward

wave. "See you later on, then."

Toby gave a small chuckle, and mirrored her wave.

"I'll miss the meeting this afternoon, probably," he said. "I'll look forward to hearing all about it."

Finn couldn't tell if he were serious or not, so she smiled politely and turned to walk back the way they had come.

"Tell Serena to send some afternoon tea, as well!" Toby yelled after her.

Finn gave another wave to show she'd heard, and continued on through the open gate and along the dirt road. She looked up at the sky. The clouds were beginning to cover more of it, moving from where they'd seemed so comfortably settled on the horizon. Now, they were closing in on the sun, and as she watched, the first wisps had drifted in front of it, making the air instantly cooler. She breathed it in with relief, and noticed how much easier the filtered light was on her eyes. She rubbed her forehead to ease her headache.

"Are you all right?" asked a voice, some short distance from her.

Finn startled, not having heard or seen anyone else since she had begun walking back from the junkyard. The person was one of those who had been in Serena's kitchen when she had arrived, an older woman with white hair and olive skin. She walked close to Finn as she spoke, peering intensely at her, as if trying to work out something. Perhaps she was simply concerned.

"I'm fine," Finn reassured her. "Just heading back to Serena's house. Toby needs some help with… something in the yard."

This seemed to satisfy the woman, who smiled. She had straight teeth, and her wrinkles fell into their well-worn laughter lines.

"I'll join you," she said, linking her arm through Finn's without giving her any chance to protest. Finn felt her usual unease at having someone she didn't know in such close quarters, but she also didn't want to risk upsetting the other woman.

"The weather's coming in," said the woman, as she took up a brisk pace. Finn's muscles, still stiff, protested, but she didn't know how to slow down without seeming awkward, so she simply kept up. "I'm Judith, by the way. It's lovely to have you back in Seven Rivers."

"Thank you…" Finn mumbled.

"I think we're in for a storm," Judith continued. "Haven't had a good rain yet this season, so this is going to be the break we've been looking for, I reckon. I suppose that'll be something new for you, having lived so long in the City?"

She looked up at Finn, her dark eyes again peering and questioning. Finn shifted her gaze to the clouds to avoid the eye contact.

"Yes, we don't get the weather like you do, here," she agreed.

"Well, you've got that to get used to now," said Judith. "And I suppose we're yet to see what will happen to the City when... well, we'll see what will happen!"

It was obvious that Judith was talking about the attack on the City but didn't seem to want to say it out loud. Finn opened her mouth to ask exactly what she meant, but Judith continued.

"I'd better get to the meeting point, then," she said. She let go of Finn's arm and patted her on the hand. "I'll see you there? Good to meet up with you again, Finn."

She walked off, quick strides on short, sturdy legs. Finn shook her head and folded her arms. Once again, she wondered how little she knew, compared to everyone else.

Perhaps the meeting would enlighten her.

She realised she was almost at Serena and Toby's house. Judith's quick pace had made the walk back much faster. Finn walked up the wooden steps and pushed open the front door just as Serena was opening it from the other side.

"You just caught me on my way out!" Serena said, brightly. "Where's Toby?"

"It was a bit too warm and sunny for me... he sent me back to get some help," Finn said. "He said you'd know who to send."

"Hmm, he probably means Allie and Haman. No problem. I'll send someone to find them, if they're not at the meeting. Anything else? You look a bit worn out."

"I feel a bit worn out. I just met Judith and she walks... very quickly."

Serena laughed.

"She does. She's one of the Elders, has been here since the beginning."

She stepped aside so that Finn could come into the house.

"I've just made tea. Why don't you sit and drink some

while I finish gathering everything together? Then we can go over to the meeting."

"Jhara?" Finn asked, feeling relief at the cool darkness in the kitchen. She sat gratefully down on a chair and poured herself a mug of tea from the pot on the table.

"Sleeping," replied Serena. "She still has a lot of healing to do, Finn. I've sent word for Eleanor to come and sit in here while we're at the meeting, so Jhara has someone to help her if she wakes while we're out."

Serena picked up a notebook which looked like it had been around since before the Collapse, and tapped her fingers on the table as she looked around the room.

"Now, what was I..." she muttered. "Ah, that's right."

She reached into the cabinet where Toby had found his tools, and pulled out another book.

"Can't forget the minutes!" she smiled.

Finn sipped her tea and took a breath.

"Serena," she began.

Serena sat, and looked at Finn closely.

"What's on your mind?"

Finn paused before continuing.

"Both Judith and Toby mentioned staying here – living

here – after the attack on the City. And I just wondered... all of this –" she waved her hand around, gestured to the books on the table near Serena's elbow " – I feel as if there is a lot I don't know. Things that have been planned which I don't know. And I... worry."

Serena's expression was kind, as usual, but not condescending, as Finn had feared.

"There is a lot you don't know. That was important, given that it was risky to send you out from the City and not know if you would make it. If PlanetRescue had decided to come after you, then we didn't want our entire operation to be revealed."

"We wouldn't have – " Finn interrupted.

"I know, I know," Serena reassured her. "I know it is not something you would ever do willingly. But don't forget, we have a lot of experience with PlanetRescue. They have some truly awful methods of extracting information. So it was safer for you and us if you knew less."

"But risky, still?"

"Oh, always. Always risky," agreed Serena. "This whole endeavour is risky. But we can't let them continue. They will end it all. We will have no other option but to assimilate with them, to become part of the City. They have done it with all the other communities and we are all that's left."

Serena suddenly looked much sadder, and more serious.

"If we allow that, then most of us will die, Finn. We are too old for the City. Too racially impure. Too different."

She breathed a deep breath, steadying herself.

"We have to fight them, at least," she continued. "Even if we don't win."

She picked up her books.

"Are you ready?" she said. "The others will be waiting, and so will Toby. I guess he's probably wondering what's happened to his helpers!"

"Oh," said Finn, putting down her mug. "He also said he wanted some afternoon tea."

"Haha!" cackled Serena. "Does he now? My nephew, the bottomless pit. He can come and make his own when he gets back. I'll pass that message on with Haman."

She grinned and held the door open for Finn, and then shut it behind them.

Chapter 6

As they walked into the meeting point, Finn could hear the hum of voices, more people than had been in Serena's kitchen. She felt the cool creep of nerves in her belly. Serena seemed to realise, and gave Finn a quick, gentle pat on the shoulder.

"It'll be fine," she said softly. "You'll sit over at the side. You only need to say something if you want to. I've got this."

Finn nodded and followed her into the dimly lit building. Inside, there were more people than she had expected; it seemed as if the whole community were there. Serena gently touched the arm of a lean, dark haired young man who was sat near the entrance, and murmured something. He grinned and nodded, then stood and gave Finn a brief smile before heading out the door.

"That's Haman," said Serena. Finn thought she recognised him from before, when Toby had walked back to the truck.

Serena continued to the front of the room, while Finn trailed a short way behind. The building was much larger than the others Finn had seen, but it was still smaller than the workspaces in the City. People were sitting on stools, chairs, cushions, or just on the wooden floor. Finn breathed in the smell of people, now beginning to seem familiar.

As Serena reached the front of the room, the murmurs of voices grew softer. Heads turned to face her, eyes focused on her, clearly interested in what she had to say. Serena placed the books and paper she had been carrying on a table and stood, hands clasped in front of her, waiting for quiet.

"Thank you all for coming," she said. Her voice was raised slightly, but still the same, friendly tone. She was obviously used to doing this.

"I know most – probably all – of you are aware that Finn and Jhara arrived in Seven Rivers two nights ago. And you'll all know that this is the signal for us to begin preparations to move in on the City."

There was some muttering here and there. Finn looked around, trying to work out who was talking, and what they were saying. She chewed on her lip, wondering if this was connected to the altercation with the fishermen. Serena, however, either ignored the noise or couldn't hear it. Either way, she continued.

"We have been preparing for this day for years. While we may have, at times, questioned whether it would ever come, the truth is, we're ready. We will set off tomorrow morning, as planned. We expect it will be two days' walk. The provisions are ready, so all that is needed today is for you to prepare your tents and ensure that your plants and animals have sufficient water and food. As previously discussed, some are staying behind to care for the community, and water gardens and tend to livestock. You know who you are. The rest of you are needed in the attack."

This time, there was no sound, no dissent, but no cheers or calls of agreement, either. Finn looked around at the crowd. Everyone seemed very serious.

"Obviously the Resistance in Western City will be ready. Finn has been working on restoring our link to the World so that we can let other Cities know their time is now. We expect to make contact tonight."

Finn felt the gaze of several sets of eyes, before the audience gave their attention back to Serena.

"The Underground will make the first strikes," continued Serena. "That will allow us to arrive and offer reinforcements, and it'll mean that PlanetRescue will be occupied with them while we travel, so we don't have to worry about transports or drones spotting us on the way. It's important we maintain a steady pace. We need to time this perfectly."

"You said transports won't be a worry." Finn heard a sceptical voice from the middle of the room.

"We'll still need to be aware, of course," admitted Serena. "That's why Braithe and friends will be doing their job inside the dome, to keep the rescuers busy. We don't need them sending out any... welcome parties."

Serena looked around the room.

"Does anyone have anything to add? Any more questions?" Serena asked.

For a moment, there was nothing. But then, a young man raised his hand and stood up. Finn recognised the men sitting next to him – the ones from the river.

"I know you say we've been preparing for this for years," he began, "but isn't an attack on the City simply poking the sleeping dragon? We're doing fine – Seven Rivers is a flourishing, contented community. Why cause trouble when we're not being directly threatened? They leave us alone, we leave them alone, right?"

There were some grunts of agreement from around the

room. Serena nodded in acknowledgement.

"It's a good point to raise," she said. "And you're right that they are not directly affecting us, at this time. But your analogy is also a good one – the sleeping dragon. One day, the sleeping dragon will wake up. And if we do nothing now, then when it does, what's to stop it from destroying us?"

"You have no proof of that, though," said another voice. It was the fisherman. "Your plan is based on a scenario you've decided is going to happen. There's no proof it will. We could be waking the dragon, as you put it, for no reason at all – and there's no knowing what mood it'll be in when we do."

"The dragon has already destroyed other communities, Alistair," said another voice, and Finn was surprised that she recognised it. Someone stood up at the other side of the room, near the front, and Finn strained to see who it was. But when the woman began to speak again, there was no doubt.

"You know as well as I do that happened to Forestdale and Sacred Springs and Sheoak Grove," said Judith. "Just hoping that PlanetRescue will spare us for some illogical reason is both cowardly and foolhardy. I would have expected more from you."

Alistair seemed to be taken aback by such a public scolding, and was surprised into silence. Judith nodded and gestured for Serena to continue, and then sat back down in her seat.

"Anyone else...?" asked Serena, managing to keep the smile from her expression, but not quite from her voice. "Well, then... I think that's it from me. Thank you again."

Finn watched as the people shifted in their seats, some getting up straight away, others turning to chat to their neighbours. She looked back at Serena, who was shuffling through the papers she had brought, and Finn thought about the way she had turned the audience to her. Finn realised she had managed to work both sides of the crowd, by allowing everyone to talk who wanted to, and softening both opposing views. Finn had a new respect for Serena. She was confident and unafraid of the challenges, unlike Finn.

Serena caught Finn's eye and smiled.

"Well? That wasn't too painful, right?"

Finn shrugged.

"I think by now, Haman and Allie will be back with Toby. Hopefully they will have been able to get what you needed. Is there anything else?

Finn described the sorts of connections and cables she would need, and Serena leant back against the table and tapped the edge of it with her right hand.

"I can… probably get something from one of the old radios. I'll talk to Avar, he maintains them."

By now, everyone else had left the room, taking with them their chairs and cushions. It was quiet and empty, and Serena and Finn's footsteps echoed off the walls.

"I come in here to get away," Serena said softly, looking around. The light was filtered through the skylight, more dimly now that the clouds had covered the sun. "It's quiet… we don't use it much, apart from meeting or social events. So I can usually guarantee I'll be alone."

Finn studied her expression, and Serena smiled, perhaps feeling a little awkward.

"I guess you have the opposite problem in the City," she said. "You are alone a lot, right?"

"There is an emphasis on spending time by yourself," Finn admitted. "I like it. I know Braithe and Jhara like to spend time together. But PlanetRescue encourages solitude. They say it's important to keep the focus on our work."

"And here, we think it helps to focus on our work if we do

spend time together."

"Does it? PlanetRescue says that solitude minimises conflict. Conflict reduces productivity."

"What do you think, though?" asked Serena. "Which way is best? Ours or theirs?"

Finn was quiet for a moment, struck by Serena's use of "ours", including her in Seven Rivers, not in the City.

"Does either one have to be perfect? I mean…"

Finn ran her thumb along her lip, trying to find the right words.

"I know that PlanetRescue has done some awful things. But we were fed, and we had shelter, and something to do with our time. I just… they could have left us to die."

"But that's exactly the point."

Serena smiled, but there was an edge to her voice.

"They did leave some of us to die," she continued. "They worked out who would be the best candidates for their City and they took them. The rest of us were left in the Badlands and they did nothing. I believe they wanted us to die. When we didn't, they began to take from us. I'm serious when I say that this is the last chance for us. You understand that, don't you?"

"I do," Finn said. "I just…"

"Make no mistake –" Serena put her hand on Finn's shoulder "– they would have sent you away if it had not been for Braithe. You can say that they gave you basic needs, but they only did that in order to keep you alive for as long as you were productive. What happens to the elderly? The sick? The disabled?"

Finn thought about the entry she had read in the diaries about enforced euthanasia, and opened her mouth to ask about it, but Serena continued.

"PlanetRescue lacks compassion. They don't care. They're only invested in you as much as they need to be, no more. Is that the kind of community you want to live in?"

"It's the kind I've always lived in," Finn said. "I don't remember any different. If you're asking me if Seven Rivers is perfect, I can't agree."

"Oh, it's not perfect by any means!" laughed Serena. "We have our problems and we don't always work them out in the best way. I feel as though we…"

She stopped and paused for long enough that Finn looked over to her. Serena seemed to be struggling with the words.

"Finn, I don't know if we can ever be perfect. Humans evolve just like everything else. So I suppose all I can say is that we're trying and we want to do better. But we're not willing to sacrifice human rights to do it. Does that seem reasonable?"

By now they had walked to the doorway. Finn looked out and up at the sky. The clouds had darkened, and were rolling into each other, clamouring for space. There was a deep boom near the horizon.

"How about we talk later?" Serena said, putting a guiding hand on Finn's shoulder. "It's going to pour. Can you smell it? The rain – that smell before it arrives... it's one of my favourite smells."

Finn sniffed but couldn't appreciate what Serena meant. She smiled and nodded anyway, hoping she seemed sincere.

"Quick, we'll get to the house. This storm looks like it could be bigger than we thought. I'll have to do some checks and make sure everything's tied down, and see some people."

She gave Finn a final pat on the back and reached to pull the door closed behind them. A gust of wind pushed it out of her hands and she laughed in surprise.

"You'd better hurry up and get inside," she said to Finn, taking a firmer grasp of the door this time. "Toby and the others should be back with your materials to make the dish. I'll meet you at the house later."

Finn put her head down against the strengthening wind and walked towards Serena's house.

She pushed on the door and had to give several shoves before it eventually relented. Eleanor was waiting on the other side and helped her as she stumbled into the kitchen.

"Oof, are you OK?" Eleanor laughed. "That storm came up quick, didn't it?"

Finn nodded and helped Eleanor push the door shut behind them. Toby stood by the kitchen counter, with his friends and Jhara sitting at the table. They all looked solemn.

"Serena's not with you?" Eleanor said.

Finn shook her head.

"She went to check that everything was tied down before the storm hit."

Toby rubbed the side of his face. Finn couldn't read his expression. Discomfort? Worry?

"We just got a message from Avar. The settlement to the

east – Bright Falls – they've asked for our help. They were raided. They need supplies."

Finn wondered why it was up to Seven Rivers to get involved. She'd never heard of Bright Falls until today. Why was it their problem? Surely Seven Rivers had enough troubles of their own without getting involved in anyone else's. She toyed with the idea of asking, but the door opened before she could speak.

"Avar just caught up with me," said Serena, a little breathless, and followed inside by a man Finn hadn't met. She assumed he was Avar.

"I'm calling a council meeting. Haman and Allie, perhaps it'd be best if you leave us for a while. This is something we need the Elders to decide."

Toby looked as if he wanted to argue, but Haman and Allie had already stood up, nodded to Serena and headed towards the door.

"Toby, I need you to get word to the Elders. Avar will come with you. We need to make a decision immediately… this couldn't have come at a worse time."

Serena sat down, folded her arms, and sighed. Toby and Avar left without a word. Finn felt uneasy at the obvious change in atmosphere.

"It's as if they know," Serena said.

"Who?" asked Finn.

"We've been having trouble with raiders for years – they're nomads, just groups of bandits I suppose, with no community. But they've been quiet lately. I'd hoped that something might have taken them out. A storm or something. We've never known where they were based and we didn't have the spare people to look. But now it looks like they're back. And right when we need everyone here..."

She shrugged.

"Well, we'll just have to do what we can. Finn, I'll ask you to stay for the meeting. I think it's important for you to hear what the Elders will have to say."

Finn waited to see whether Serena would give some clue as to what that might be, but Serena simply filled the kettle from the small tank on the bench, and put it on the stove, stoking the fire underneath it.

Jhara caught Finn's eye and raised her eyebrows in question, but Finn wasn't sure what expression was the right response. There was an awkward silence. Serena usually seemed relaxed and chatty with the Elders but now she busied herself with the teapot instead of talking. The wind rattled the walls and windows. When the door opened again, Finn felt relieved at the distraction the new people brought.

Judith held onto the door tightly against the wind, and the first of the Elders stepped into the kitchen. Toby and Avar must have run. Finn tightened her fists to try and release some of the tension. Serena looked over and nodded with a taut smile at the Elders, then continued to pour tea.

People murmured to each other while they waited. Everyone seemed unsettled; Finn felt her anxiety building. There were too many people there. The room became stifling and Finn had to concentrate on her breathing. She wondered if would draw too much attention if she left, but at the same time, she didn't want to miss what Serena or the others said.

The door flung open again and Toby and Avar stepped back through. Their hair was wet and there were large dark spots on their clothes where the heavy drops had hit. The rain had begun. Finn inhaled and realised Serena had been right – it did smell different. Like dirt, as if it had mixed with the air.

Behind Avar were three more Elders, stepping carefully over the threshold. Toby held the door open for them and once they were through, closed it and leant with his back against it. Serena turned and looked at the small gathering.

"Thanks for making it at such short notice. We have some new information which I wanted to discuss with you."

Finn closed her eyes.

"Bright Falls has been raided and has sent a request for help. We need to make a choice as to whether we send it, or go ahead with our plan."

For a long moment, nobody spoke, then Judith looked around.

"We can't do both?" she said.

Serena let out a long sigh.

"It would stretch our resources out too much. There is…" she rubbed her eyes, "…so much uncertainty. We don't know what will happen once we get to the City. We don't know whether there'll be any retaliation."

"I thought you said that problem would be taken care of from the inside? Braithe was supposed to be organising it?"

This was from a man Finn didn't recognise, but his voice seemed kind enough. She saw Jhara look up at the mention of Braithe's name.

"She is, Eli. But we can't be sure – nothing is certain.

And Bright Falls needs help now. Raiders may come back."

"So in that case, we don't risk it," said Eli, firmly. "We go ahead with the plan. We head through to the City. We make sure it falls. Then some of us go over to Bright Falls and help, once we're done."

"But that might be too late!" protested Judith. She seemed indignant at the suggestion.

"If we go now and stretch ourselves too thin, then we might lose our chance," said Eli. His voice was quiet, but he had conviction.

"This was why I needed you all here," said Serena. "You can understand the dilemma."

Again, quiet.

Serena spoke again: "We can carry out our original plan. Or help Bright Falls and hope that we'll be able to still go through with the run on the City once we've helped them. Do we want to discuss it, or just vote?"

Finn admired the way Serena cut to the chase, seeming to read the group, sensing that the discussion could go on for hours if she didn't stop it.

There was another short pause before anyone spoke.

"I don't see me changing my mind," Eli said. "Why don't

we just vote?"

Most other heads nodded.

"All right then." Serena clasped her hands together in front of her. Was she nervous, Finn wondered?

"If you agree that we should travel to help Bright Falls before marching on the City, raise your hand."

Finn counted six hands. Judith's and Serena's were among them. Eli and two others kept theirs resting in their laps. Eli glanced around and sighed.

"Well, we have some organising to do," Serena said. "Avar, I need you to see if you can contact our people in the City. Toby, the truck?"

"It's ready."

"You'll just need a little food and water, and rations in case of emergency. So you'll have plenty of room for provisions for Bright Falls. Take an extra battery. We don't want to have to send out a search party if you run out of power."

She stood up.

"This is what we do best – innovate and mobilise. It's how we've lasted this long. While Toby's away, we'll just continue with our preparations."

The Elders sat and talked quietly and Jhara hoisted herself up on her crutches to walk over towards Finn. Finn realised her expectations that these people might jump straight into action was unrealistic – the youngest of them would have been in their sixties. As Jhara reached Finn's side, Toby suddenly also appeared next to her.

"She'll send you with me," he said softly to Finn, but loud enough for Jhara to hear as well.

Finn looked at him.

"What? Who will? Where?"

"Serena," mumbled Toby. "To Bright Falls. I'll bet it."

The Elders were standing up now, talking with Serena and nodding. Even Eli was engaged. After a few moments, they began to leave, and Serena beckoned Finn, Jhara and Toby over to her.

"I need to talk to you all," she said to all of us as she pulled out a chair at the table and indicated they should do the same.

"Finn," she said, when they were seated, "I want you to go along with Toby."

"Told you so," Toby muttered.

"You what?" asked Serena.

"I said you'd want her along. Had a feeling."

"Well, aren't you the psychic?" said Serena, drily. "Anyway, Toby will need a travelling companion for safety – it's important to have an extra pair of eyes out there."

She paused for a moment and Finn looked up to catch her eye. It was as if Serena wanted to say something else, and Finn waited, but when Serena said nothing, Finn spoke up.

"What about the dish?" she asked. "We have everything we need to construct it. Wouldn't it be better if I stayed here? I'm happy to work through the night."

Serena looked around the room. Judith was the last Elder to leave. Serena waited until she had closed the door before she spoke again.

"Finn, it is getting dangerous now. I don't have many people I know I can trust."

She rubbed her eyes with her fingers and kept her hands pressed against her face as she sighed.

"I need you to go because I know I can trust you. And I hoped that they might not have been cut off from the World yet. If they haven't you might be able to get through quicker. It could make all the difference."

"What did they say when they contacted Avar?" Toby asked.

"Not much. To be truthful, we don't have a great relationship with them but it's been a case of sticking together since PlanetRescue began their recent purges."

"I would have thought there would have been more solidarity?" Jhara said.

"Disaster doesn't always bring people together," Serena replied. "Scarcity can breed a fear... of more scarcity, I suppose."

She shrugged as if signalling that the conversation was over, and turned to Toby.

"You can leave straight away?"

He raised his eyebrows.

"You don't want to wait until morning?"

"Time is not our friend at the moment. We need to get you back as soon as we can."

He shrugged and stood.

"OK. You ready, Finn?"

Finn looked over at Jhara, who nodded.

"I'll be fine," said Jhara.

Finn smiled in return, guilty that she hadn't considered

whether Jhara would miss her or even really worried about Jhara's well-being. She was more concerned about herself and being alone with only one other person for several hours. Toby had given her no reason to distrust him, and she liked him well enough, but people were difficult. One person on their own was difficult. But there was no way out of it without confrontation and having to explain herself. So she stood, and shrugged, trying to appear nonchalant.

"I'm ready."

"Toby and Avar will load the truck. If you want to grab anything to take, now's the time."

Finn almost laughed in reply. What would she take? It wasn't as if she had any belongings.

"I'm OK," she said to Serena. "I'll go and help."

Jhara struggled to her feet again, and grabbed Finn's arm.

"Be careful."

"I will."

Avar opened the door and the smell of rain swept into the kitchen. Finn shivered with the sudden change of temperature, and then with a last look at Jhara, she followed Avar and Toby out into the storm.

Chapter 7

Finn sat on the ground near the shed at the edge of the town. Toby had parked the truck up close to it so they only had to shift supplies a short distance from where they were stacked neatly in the shed. It had taken less than half an hour to pack the truck; it would have been quicker but for the gusts of wind which flicked up the tarpaulin as they struggled to pack provisions under it. Eventually, the truck was full – Finn was surprised that Serena and the Elders had decided to give away so much.

"Well, it's an 'I scratch your back and you scratch mine'," explained Toby when she questioned it. "You know. They'll help out when we need it, hopefully."

Finn was about to ask more, but Avar walked over, carrying a large metal box.

"Forget something?" he said, hefting the box into Toby's chest. "Where would you be without me, huh? I'll bet you even promised Serena you'd pack an extra battery."

"I think I promised her I'd take two," grinned Toby.

He shifted the box to a raised knee so he could open the truck door with one hand, and slid the battery up onto the seat.

"We'll sort it out when we get in," he said to Finn. "You can probably rest your feet on it."

They heard a voice in the dark and turned to peer at a figure walking up the dirt road.

"I've just come to make sure you leave," called Serena as she came within view.

"Typical. Not 'good luck' or 'be careful,'" Toby laughed. "Just 'go away.'"

"Good luck. Be careful," she said, putting her arms around him and squeezing tightly. She smiled, too, but there was something else in her expression that Finn couldn't quite interpret. Serena let Toby out of her embrace and turned to Finn.

"Be safe, Finn. We'll look forward to seeing you back as soon as possible. Let's hope this trip is... successful."

Finn hoped her smile seemed genuine. All of this – the walk to Seven Rivers, Jhara's injury, the food, the so-many people – had been a grating background disturbance, a constant irritation that nothing was how it should be. Too much newness, too much unpredictability. And no control. She wished again that she had never jumped out of the vent with Jhara. Now she was about to leave once more, against her better judgement, to help people she didn't know on behalf of people she barely knew. Why had she ever agreed to this?

"Well," Serena said. She held out her hand to press palms with Finn. Finn put her own out in return and they touched.

"See you soon," said Toby, interrupting the silence.

"Yes."

Serena held Finn's gaze for a moment longer, the wind whipping her hair in front of her face.

"Yes," she repeated. "See you soon."

She raised her arm in farewell and went to stand next to Avar in the doorway of the goods shed.

Finn pulled on the stiff handle of the truck door and grunted with the effort it took to open it. Toby was already in the driver's seat as she hauled herself up, sliding onto the cool vinyl.

"Ready to go?" asked Toby, his teeth grinning white in the low light.

"No," said Finn, "but let's go anyway."

The way out of Seven Rivers was wet from the storm and

Finn saw Toby clenching his jaw as the truck skidded slowly to the sides of the road, and he guided it back into the grooves in the track. Finn was glad for the distraction, as frightening as it was to be sliding in such a large vehicle. She held on tightly to the door handle and gripped the edge of the seat, the cracks in the vinyl digging into her hand.

After several minutes, the road improved; the storm which had drenched Seven Rivers had taken a different direction and the sand was heaped up at the sides of the track in soft dry mounds. Finn glanced across at Toby. He seemed to have relaxed.

"So," he said, with a quick glance in her direction. "You're quiet."

"I'm not ever noisy."

Finn felt her annoyance rise in her chest as Toby let out a bark of laughter.

"I mean you're not talking much. What are you thinking?"

Finn considered whether she wanted to share her thoughts with him. He did seem to be willing to disagree with Serena and the others in Seven Rivers, but she didn't know if it would be too much of a challenge if she told him what she really thought.

"Not much at all. It's a bit frightening being out here at night," she said. It was only half a lie. It wasn't just being out at night, but also the danger than PlanetRescue might send someone after them, since they were out there all on their own.

"Well, there's not much out here to kill you," Toby grinned. "And Bright Falls isn't too far away. If we can keep at this pace we'll be there by midnight."

"So soon?" Finn asked.

"We are going about 70 kays an hour," Toby said. "Kilometres, I mean."

"I understood the abbreviation. It's OK."

"Anyway – the truck can go a bit faster but I want to be able to stop if there's a pothole or something."

"Or something?" Finn asked.

"Raiders sometimes."

Finn looked at him and sighed as she saw his mouth twitching.

"You're taking advantage of my lack of knowledge," she said.

"Sorry. We almost certainly won't see Raiders. But I am a bit nervous. I've only been over to Bright Falls a few times, never at night, and with communications down, it's a bit… scary."

Finn studied his expression, but he did seem genuinely anxious.

"So I am right to be frightened."

"No," he said, more loudly than seemed necessary. "I mean, maybe a bit. We should be fine. Serena wouldn't have sent us if she didn't think it was safe."

Finn shifted back in her seat, watching as the lights from the truck bounced against trees, rocks, bushes. Nature seemed to leap out as the light touched and then, just as quickly, slip back into the darkness as they drove further into the night.

"I put some food behind the seat for us," Toby said. "I figured we might need something since we missed out on dinner, with all that was going on."

Finn realised that he was indicating for her to get it, and she knelt on the seat, holding onto it as the vibrations from the road shuddered through her knees. There was a fabric bag with handles, leaning against the side of the cab, and she hooked her fingers under it, hauling it towards her.

"Plenty there," said Toby as Finn settled back in her seat

again. "Take what you want and I'll have the rest."

Finn rummaged through and found some rice balls wrapped in a thin towel. She bit into one, tentatively. It was cool and lumpy, tasting of salt and perhaps garlic, but edible. At least it would be something solid in her stomach.

"There's tea, too," Toby said, handing her a flask.

Finn smiled her thanks and took it from him, but waited until she had eaten her rice ball before she opened it.

"Weird, I guess, how we call it tea," said Toby as she tried her first swig. "I remember tea from when I was really little. And it was nothing like this. I think this one is lemongrass and raspberry leaf. But the tea Serena used to drink when I was little... that was something only adults were allowed – or maybe teens. And you added milk and sugar. Oh, and then there was coffee..."

He sounded excited and Finn wanted to chuckle at his enthusiasm.

"I used to love the smell of coffee. Serena, too. Haven't seen any of it since I was about ten."

Finn steadied the flask as she unwound the lid, then poured some of the tea into a wooden cup. Some splashed onto her fingers; it was lukewarm, not hot. Perhaps whoever had made it – Serena, maybe? – had thought about how difficult it would be to pour in the truck as it slipped and jolted along the track. She managed to wind the lid back on one-handed and sipped the warm liquid as best she could. After a moment she realised that there was a silence that others might interpret as uncomfortable. Braithe had warned her about this. Finn found small talk so pointless but Braithe had insisted they practise. She thought back to the kinds of questions she had rehearsed.

"You were young when you came to Seven Rivers, yes?"

Toby looked over at her as if he were surprised at the question, and for a second, Finn worried that it might have been inappropriate. But then he smiled and shrugged.

"I think I was about five or six when we moved here? I don't really remember much before that. We travelled around a lot. Apparently things were pretty bad depending on where you were. So Serena had to keep moving to keep us both safe."

"Serena's not your mother, though."

"That's right, she's my auntie. My mum – her sister – died when I was a baby. There was nobody to look after me so Serena took care of me." He paused. "We were living in

Sydney before the Collapse."

"Serena said she was in Sydney then." Finn frowned, remembering the images and audio she had seen of the city when it fell. Looting and violence, murders... it had been one of the cities hardest hit, mostly because so many had flocked there in the preceding years. It was a mega city, and when it exploded, the shockwaves in other centres were palpable. Sydney had been the canary in the coal mine, as they used to say. Shame they hadn't paid attention to actual canaries in actual coalmines, Finn thought. Everything could have been different.

"She doesn't talk about it much," Toby said, interrupting Finn's train of thought. "But I think it really had an impact. I mean, I don't know. I don't even remember life without her – I was only a few months old when she got me. And you know what it was like, well, we hear stories about whole families disappearing and I don't even know where we came from."

"Serena doesn't talk about it? Her family?"

Toby shook his head.

"Maybe she thinks she's protecting me, but I've learnt as much as I can on my own about it. I'd like to know something about where I come from. Who my people are."

Finn linked her hands together and stared at her fingernails, remembering what both Serena and Eleanor had said about the residents of Seven Rivers finding their people, their family, in the community. But Toby had lived almost all his life there. He had a community, and wanted more. She understood that ache. Out of the corner of her eye, she saw Toby put both hands on the wheel as the truck slid to the side of the road, but he guided it back into the tracks, and smiled back over at Finn.

"This sand's keeping me on my toes."

Finn wasn't sure if he had driven into the sand on purpose to avoid talking more about his childhood and his yearning for answers, but whatever the cause, the moment seemed to have passed, and they rode in silence for a while.

"I wondered," Toby said softly, "about music. It's such a part of life for us in Seven Rivers. We sing and play together. We have a kind of orchestra – about once a month, we hold a concert. But you guys don't – didn't – have that in the City, right? Seems so strange to me."

Finn shook her head. She realised he had changed subject on purpose, but didn't mind.

"There is music. We have the whole World. You can hear

whatever you want – the history of music, the catalogue of everything humans have produced is in there."

"But playing it with your own hands," Toby insisted. "I mean, actually making music, with other people."

"It's not something that happens. It's discouraged," Finn admitted. "I don't think it makes so much difference."

"Between live music and recorded? Oh, Finn. You haven't lived until you've heard live music."

He glanced over at her and smiled an odd smile, and Finn felt uncomfortable, the irritation rising up in her as it had done so often over the last few days. Everyone in Seven Rivers had had this same attitude, a kind of condescension. Even Jhara seemed convinced, so ready to throw her lot in with Serena and all the others, so ready to give up on everything in the City.

"How are you certain that your world is the best one?" Finn blurted out, and Toby stared at her for so long that she was concerned the truck might veer into the trees.

"The whole thing," Finn continued, "this entire time has been about you all. So sure of yourselves. Ready to bring down PlanetRescue. Everyone's just so – " Finn struggled to find the words she wanted " – *mean* about the City. And none of you have even been there."

She took a shuddering breath, as quietly as she could, hoping it wasn't possible to tell how fast her heart was beating.

There was another silence while they both stared straight ahead at the meagre glow cast by the headlights of the truck onto the sandy grey road.

Eventually, when Toby spoke, it was in a much gentler tone.

"I didn't really think about it. I'm sorry, Finn. The City was your home."

"It still is," said Finn. "I don't know any different. I don't really want to. I *want* to go back, even though I know it's going to change."

"You don't want to go through with the attack?" said Toby. She could hear the worry creeping into his voice.

"I know we have to. I know PlanetRescue has to be stopped. I know they've done awful things. It just... isn't so simple. It's not as simple as everyone seems to think."

With difficulty, she met his eyes and was surprised to see him nodding.

"You're absolutely right. It's not simple at all. I suppose

we are just fighting back. You have to understand, they are taking everything away. Everything. It's not just the people – that's bad enough. It's the whole story of the country. That means something. They're destroying *everything*."

His voice cracked and Finn thought he was gripping the steering wheel tighter than before. She expected him to say more but instead he stared ahead, lips grimly pressed together.

She laced her fingers together and breathed out slowly and quietly. She had lost her temper, and now, according to what Braithe had taught her, she needed to apologise.

"I'm sorry," she said, making sure it was loud enough for him to hear her. Toby shrugged in response and Finn frowned. He was supposed to say something back. This wasn't how the script worked.

"I am, too," he said, eventually. "I *don't* know anything about the City. You're right."

He looked over at her with a small smile.

"Tell me about the World. What's it like?"

"It's..." Finn struggled to describe it. Being inWorld was an immersive experience. It filled the senses, it gave comfort and connection, answered every need, every question. But how to explain that to somebody who had never known it, and who seemed to never want to know it?

"It's like being in a dream where everything is real," she said, finally. "It's hard to tell you if you've not ever been there. It's like this –" she gestured around them " – but with all the knowledge of the whole of humanity. It's like being linked to everyone who lives now and everyone and everything that has ever lived."

Toby nodded, as if he could imagine it, but Finn felt like her description were still too inadequate. She was just about to expand on it when the truck lurched forward into a sudden stop. Finn felt her body fold around the seatbelt and she gasped at the shock.

"What…" she began, looking at Toby, but his thin-lipped expression had changed into one of bright excitement.

"Look," he whispered, touching her briefly on the shoulder and pointing out the windscreen.

Finn peered into the pool of light on the sand and saw nothing, but then something moved just beyond where the headlights were shining – a figure, its eyes reflecting the light of the truck.

"It's…" she squinted, unsure.

"It's a 'roo," Toby finished in a low voice.

He flicked a dial and the headlights blinked out. Finn opened her eyes wide, trying to adjust to the dark. After a moment, she could see shapes of the bushes and some taller trees, off to the side of the track, and then she looked ahead again at the kangaroo.

In the dimness, she could see the animal's ears turning, cupping the air from all around, identifying the direction of sounds. Otherwise, it stayed very still, its front paws, small arms, hanging down in front of its chest. It sat on its haunches as if it were almost relaxed, leaning on that thick tail. But as Finn adjusted in her seat to lean forward, the kangaroo also shifted, and Finn realised it was anything but relaxed. It was poised, all muscles taut and ready, its legs tightly sprung to send it into the bushes to hide.

Toby put his arm out towards her, as if holding her back.

"Just watch," he said, voice barely a murmur.

They both stared straight ahead as the kangaroo peered back at them, its ears still swivelling slowly. Finn tried to be as quiet as she could, barely breathing. She glanced over at Toby, but he was leaning over the steering wheel, eyes fixed on the creature as it tried to locate them, and perhaps decipher who they were.

As Finn turned back, the kangaroo startled, looking behind, and then with unexpected speed, it leapt straight over to the side of the track and bounded into the bush.

Finn exhaled, finally, and found herself smiling.

"Pretty incredible, eh?" said Toby, his eyes and teeth shining in the dark.

"Yeah," said Finn. "Pretty incredible."

"That's what it's about, you see," he said, flicking on the lights again and turning the key in the ignition. "It's them. 'Roos and everything. The country. Everything. You can't have this if you're in a bubble. They can't recreate this inWorld. If we lose this, it's gone forever. What's left?"

Finn shrugged, but Toby obviously did not expect an answer, since he continued on with barely a pause.

"Did I ever tell you about the time I got in between two 'roos? Stupid. I mean, I was stupid. They were fighting and I'd known them for years. We used to see the group out near the outskirts of Seven Rivers when I was on garden rotation. Anyway, I spotted a Raider over to the side, with a rifle. He was going to shoot these two bucks. I mean, I know we all need to eat. But these were our 'roos. So I went in, to break them up, and get in the way of the gun. Serena was so upset when she found out."

He grinned at the memory.

"So I ran over and normally, the 'roos would scatter at a human running towards them, but these guys knew us, so they were pretty tame. One just turned to me, massive big guy. Pushed his shoulder back and his chest out, and drew himself up tall. I guessed he was about to lean back on his tail and kick me so I just ran in towards him, shoulder into his chest, elbow in his belly and it was enough to catch him by surprise. They both jumped away and I ran, too… didn't want the Raider to start shooting at me."

Finn nodded. There was probably some socially appropriate response but she didn't know what it was. Talking suddenly seemed exhausting and more unnecessary than usual. She shrugged. Luckily, Toby seemed happy with the silence, too, and they continued on the track, as usual the wheels sometimes shifting in the sand, and gliding the truck to the side. Always, though, Toby was able to gently guide the vehicle back to the centre, and Finn lay her head back on the seat, the close encounter with the animal filling her mind when she closed her eyes. Such otherness.

She woke to Toby gently shaking her shoulder, and she flinched involuntarily at the unexpected touch.

"Sorry. But we're here. The settlement is just round the corner."

Finn sat up, rubbing the sleep out of one eye.

"Why aren't we around the corner, then?"

Toby frowned, as if he were trying to work out what to say.

"Rescuers."

Finn looked ahead of them; Toby had switched off the lights and the truck was idling, but there didn't seem to be any movement around them. She peered through the window to her side, but there was only dark scrub and the occasional tall tree.

"What? Where?"

Toby pointed into the trees.

"Through there. I saw the transport land."

From the back of Finn's neck, a tendril of cold fear spread over her scalp. She shuddered.

"I don't know what they're doing," Toby whispered. "But it can't be good. Can it?"

He looked as if he wanted her to reassure him, to dismiss what they both knew.

"No," she agreed," it can't."

Chapter 8

Toby had grabbed a backpack, slid out of his window, and dropped silently to the ground, but Finn knew that if she were to try the same trick, she might break a bone, or at the very least, make more noise than was desirable.

Toby ran quickly around to the passenger's side and quietly opened Finn's door. Finn sat on the edge of the truck, over the wheel, and dangled her legs down towards the ground.

"Just jump," whispered Toby. "It's soft, it's fine."

Finn held her breath and pushed herself off with her hands, landing a second later in the sand. Toby grabbed her sleeve and pulled her into the undergrowth.

He began to push aside branches as they headed deeper into the bush. They crushed wet grass and leaves underfoot and Finn breathed in the damp air. Everything smelt green and alive.

The road where they had left the truck carried on around in a wide curve, hugging the bushland. Walking in a direct line, Toby and Finn were able to shortcut through to the edge of the road on the other side. They stayed back, behind four tall trees and some undergrowth.

Bright Falls was smaller than Seven Rivers, Finn knew. She could see the shadowed outlines of buildings, but it was hard to tell how far back they stretched. But her attention was held by the transport to their left, its landing lights shining off the closest houses. A few Rescuers were walking back towards the transport.

"What are they doing?" asked Finn quietly.

Toby shrugged.

"I can't understand where all the Bright Falls residents are. There's at least fifty people living here."

"Maybe they've taken them all with them already?" Finn suggested.

"Maybe they're only planning to take a few," Toby muttered.

"Maybe," said a low voice close behind them, "the transport's for you."

Toby and Finn whipped around to see a Rescuer standing in the undergrowth. He held a stunner in his left hand, his balaclava hiding any expression. There was a hole in his uniform near his left shoulder, and Finn could see his bare skin. It seemed strange that someone so rigidly obedient to PlanetRescue would be human.

"Eva would like a word," said the Rescuer, gesturing to the transport. "Let's go."

Finn looked at Toby and tried to interpret his expression – something between fear and despair and apology. He shook his head slightly and stood up.

"We need to go with them, Finn," he said.

"You should know this operation has been ordered directly by Eva," said the Rescuer.

"Is that supposed to make us feel better?" asked Toby.

Finn pushed her hands into the dirt and grabbed a low-hanging branch for support as she stood.

"It means we can't harm you," replied the Rescuer, nudging them forwards with the end of his stunner, but it remained on safety. "No matter how stupid we think you are. Anyway, you'll be there soon enough."

Finn and Toby stumbled as they reached the edge of the bush where it met the road. The transport wasn't far but Finn felt her legs tremble as if she'd walked for hours, and a disappointment so intense it was almost grief, a longing to be able to link inWorld to contact Jhara, to get more information, anything to give her a more detailed explanation than what she saw and felt. Anything to help it make sense.

The air transport ride was short. Finn resented how quickly it travelled above the landscape she'd had to walk over with Jhara. She wanted to talk to Toby, or at least ask about the plan, now that everything had changed. But there was silence inside the transport and the Rescuers kept their balaclavas on and their stunners at the ready. For all its brevity, it was still a quiet, harrowing journey.

Finally, the transport began to hover.

"Landing," said the Rescuer who had marched them on board, his voice muffled through the covering on his face. "You two will be getting off here."

He motioned to Finn and Toby with his stunner.

The transport shook gently as its gear stretched out to settle against the ground. The Rescuer jerked his chin in their direction and Finn and Toby both stood. Finn stepped onto the ramp and moved her feet slowly down the slope until she reached the ground. She looked over at the City, shimmering under the skydome. Back where she'd started.

"Go to the council chambers," said the Rescuer. He was still standing on the ramp, and for a split second, Finn wondered if they could somehow run away, use the element of surprise to escape before the Rescuer had a chance to use his stunner. But she had no clue as to how far the weapon could reach, and even less idea about where they would go.

"Over there," said the Rescuer, pointing at the main gate.

Finn and Toby began to walk. Finn could feel the eyes of the Rescuer on her back, and sure enough, when she looked over her shoulder, he was still standing on the ramp, hands on the stunner, watching them. But at least they were out of earshot, and she could now talk to Toby.

"What are we going to do? What if Eva has us shot? What will they do with everyone else?" The questions that had been trapped inside her tumbled out in a rush.

Toby clasped her hand briefly, a quick reassuring touch.

"I don't know. I don't know. I don't... know."

He shifted the backpack onto his shoulder. The Rescuers had rummaged through its contents and seeming satisfied that they were unthreatening, had returned it to Toby on the transport flight.

"Remember what Serena said," he continued. "She has confidence in you."

Finn snorted.

"No pressure."

As they approached the gate, it opened, the huge doors sliding sideways, and with a deep breath, Finn walked through, hoping she appeared braver than she felt. It was not as comforting being back in the City as she had imagined it would be. She looked over to the council chambers. She had travelled in an autodriver everyday on the way to WorldSec, right next door. Everything looked the same, but it felt different. What had it done to her, being in the Badlands, even for only a few days?

"I can't believe they don't have more security," Toby said, looking up and down the roads. It was dark and quiet, like a normal night, which it was, Finn thought, to most of the Cityzens.

"They don't need any," Finn shrugged. "It's automated and there are cameras. And people don't need to come out at night, or want to. They feel safe in their blocks."

Toby continued to stare, looking at everything: the smooth road, the clean blocks. Finn wondered what he was so interested in, and then realised that this was all entirely new for him. He hadn't even had the benefit of seeing images of the City inWorld, as she had done with the Badlands.

Now that they were within the confines of the City, Finn welcomed the thought of connecting back into the World. She switched her thoughts to make the link but there was nothing. The reports from the Resistance the day before had been correct. No World. She gasped softly and Toby glanced at her.

"It's OK. I'm fine."

She knew she sounded like Jhara, and thought about her, and about Braithe who must be in the City somewhere. They walked over to the council block. It stood in darkness, except for the top floor, three storeys up. Someone had lit lamps. Eva, Finn thought.

There was nobody in reception. Finn and Toby walked over to the stairs.

"Can't remember ever climbing more than a few steps," Toby smiled. "I'm not sure I've ever seen a staircase like this. How strange."

Finn simply placed her foot on the first step and put her hand on the railing. The bamboo was cool to the touch.

As they reached the third floor, it seemed as quiet as the downstairs lobby, but the door to the main room in front of them stood slightly ajar. An invitation, if ever there was one.

They walked slowly towards it, and the door was pulled open from the other side. In the doorway stood a woman.

"I assume it's me you're looking for," she said. "I'm Eva. Won't you come in?"

Finn was tempted to turn and run, but it was too impractical. The Rescuers would find her.

"I'm completely alone," Eva assured them. "I have been waiting for you. I've been watching."

She gestured in at the room and they walked in to see a table and some chairs in front of glass windows which stretched from floor to ceiling. One of the windows was open, on a hinge, like a door, to give access to the balcony. Finn turned as she heard Eva close the door behind them. It felt as if an escape route were being closed off, but she forced down the anxiety and instead turned around to watch Eva walk across the room towards them.

She was a woman of small build, neither fat nor thin. She didn't have particularly unpleasant features, and her hair was white, tied back in an unpretentious bun. Everything about her was unremarkable. Finn realised she was almost disappointed. She had expected something more dramatic. Someone more overtly evil.

Eva sat in the well-worn armchair and leant her head back to look at them. She didn't offer them somewhere to sit, and so they stood, self-consciously, on the other side of the table.

"You've been busy, Finn," Eva kept eye contact for longer than Finn could stand. She looked away and felt her face redden.

"We did what we had to. You lied."

"I never lied to you,"

Eva's voice was calm, light even. She seemed so completely undisturbed by their presence and Finn hated her for it.

"You lied by omission," Toby said before Finn could speak. "You hid information. People deserve to know what really happened. The Collapse was your fault – your company's fault."

Eva paused, and in the silence, the sky outside lit up with an orange flash, and a second later, a muffled boom. Finn and Toby rushed to the balcony to see smoke rising from the outer edge of the dome. Eva remained seated.

"Your Underground. Your 'Resistance.' They're making their move. I've been waiting."

Finn walked back to the edge of the table, finally sitting in one of the empty chairs. It was smooth and comfortable, an antique from before the Collapse.

"You knew about them?"

"Of course I did," Eva scoffed. "I've known about everything. We saw all your preparations. We knew this was coming. Serena, Braithe, all of it. We got you to Bright Falls to avoid any confrontation with Seven Rivers –"

"That was you?" said Finn.

"Of course it was. We sent Rescuers to make sure the Bright Falls residents wouldn't interfere. I wanted you to be here... for this."

Eva waved her hand in the direction of the window, to the outside where Finn assumed the fire was still burning.

"I wanted you here to see it fall."

Finn furrowed her brow, confused.

"This is you," Eva continued. "It's all about you. Once we knew that Braithe was working for the Resistance, we knew we wouldn't get you back."

She sighed.

"We had high hopes for you. So clever – the cleverest any of us had ever seen. You saw WorldSec solutions before anyone else. You have a talent for the kinds of problem-solving PlanetRescue could have used. We planned to use you. Planned to make the Cities and the World so much more than they are. And instead you've brought them down."

"What makes you think she would have stuck with you?" Toby blurted out. "She's better on the side of the Badlands – she's free and she knows the truth."

"I'm right here," Finn said, indignantly, looking from one to the other. Toby seemed apologetic but Eva simply threw up her hands.

"You still think it's all about us and them. PlanetRescue versus the Badlands. But you don't know what it was like. You never lived in a world before the Collapse..."

She paused for so long that Finn wondered if she were expecting them to say something.

"I saw it coming. I hoped that humanity would change," Eva continued, eventually. "Instead it was the planet that started to change. People ignored all the warning signs. I didn't ignore them. I planned for them. I knew everything was going to go to hell and I started to prepare long before the governments. Even those doomsday preppers, they had no clue. They were preparing for an apocalypse where they could be smug, well-fed, well-armed. When ninety-five percent of the world's population is hungry and thirsty and the crops are dying, there is no such thing as well-fed, no matter how much you have stored in your bunker. There is only fear and fighting and death."

Eva folded her arms and looked down over the City.

"We had been developing technology for many years. I hired the very best. We came out with all the breakthrough tech. The skydomes, the cloud-seeding, the solar on which the City runs – even in the Badlands, they use our tech.

"Governments couldn't wait to get their hands on it. They were ready to pay any price. After the famines of '20 and '21, they were desperate. And so we began to roll it out. It took a while, but we had partnerships everywhere. I had thought of it all, you see. I knew there would come a day. After the massacres in San Francisco they were thankful of our security. If it hadn't been for us, where would humanity have gone? Descended into chaos. There would be nothing left by now. The governments needed us to keep the people in control. The people needed us because they didn't trust the government."

"You seem to have a very selective memory of what you

did," said Finn. "You say you were doing it all for the people, but where did the people get a say in this?"

"People are... stupid," Eva said, turning around again, and continuing her pacing. "They have ideas about what they want, but almost all of the time, they don't know what they actually need."

"So you decided there should be a dictatorship? With you as the ruler?" asked Toby, angrily.

"I don't think dictatorship is the word I would have used," said Eva, almost amused at his disdain. "You think a free vote is the pinnacle of everything, that it's the key. But a majority is only fifty-one percent. That means that almost half the population can be left disappointed. And those who won, what they can achieve? You think a democracy is the best we can do? You're as misguided as they were, all those years ago."

Finn was uncomfortable; she paced to the window and back again, irritated at Eva's calmness.

"But to take all the decisions out of their hands, to lie..."

"Don't be so naïve. Everyone lies. We didn't lie as much as not tell the truth. There were rumours, we just refused to clarify them. People can't be trusted to make good decisions."

"But people..." Finn struggled to find the words. "You can't just take away their power..."

"Oh, it's overrated. They don't miss it."

"But some of us didn't want that," Finn protest. "And what about the people who don't fit into your Cities? How can you justify getting rid of them?"

Finn's voice cracked, but Eva simply shrugged.

"Look at the quality of life of the Cityzens now. Everyone is well-fed. Everyone has the opportunity to work. No poverty. There is clean water, sanitation. And yet, as I said, you can't please everyone. And we couldn't please you."

Eva looked at Finn, her gaze intense, and this time Finn forced herself not to look away.

Eva smiled.

"I won't be any bother," she said, so calm it made Finn uneasy. "You think you're doing the right thing, don't you? Just know that I thought – that we thought – we were doing the right thing, too. But have you even thought about what will happen tomorrow, or the next day, or the next day? I thought about that. That's why I managed to keep it going for so long."

She stood up, and walked over to the balcony, looking over towards the fire in the distance.

"Fire," she said, her voice softer now. "There's always fire, at the end."

She turned around to glance at them, but then turned back to the window.

"It's a beautiful City," she said. "They were all beautiful Cities. I hope you can make something just as perfect. I hope you manage something like this."

And even as Finn realised what was happening, and ran forward in an attempt to stop it, Eva shifted her weight onto one arm, leapt over the balustrade, and fell silently and quickly, landing with a distant thud on the concrete below.

Chapter 9

Finn stopped short of the balustrade, reluctant to see the body which had been alive and arguing only seconds before. She turned to look at Toby, who stood back near the table, his mouth open, eyes wide.

Neither of them said anything for a moment. Outside, the noise built to a level that bothered Finn. It was the sound of chaos, of belligerence and antagonism, of confrontation. She dreaded having to be part of it. Finn suddenly felt weak. She managed to walk back to the table and then half-fell into a chair, waving away Toby's outstretched hand.

"I'm fine," she said, wondering if he could tell how often she had told this lie in the past few days. She tried again to connect inWorld, and this time, the link worked. Finn felt the joy at the familiar sense of completion, an anticipation of her consciousness locking into the expanse of other knowledge and expertise. But almost instantly, her stomach turned over as she realised that the World was empty. None of the other minds she knew, none of the colours or the information, the audio, the stories. Everything had disappeared.

It's about the whole story of the country, of everyone, of all we've ever been.

That's what Toby had meant. The history, the memories. He didn't understand the World but he had talked about the connection, and now her connection was gone, Finn felt desperately, terrifyingly alone.

"You don't look fine," said Toby, peering at her. "I'm going to get someone."

"No… please stay. I don't want to be alone in case…"

There was an explosion outside, close to the building; the windows at the balcony rattled in their frames. Toby and Finn exchanged a glance and looked around the room. There was nowhere to hide.

"We need a weapon – something!" said Toby, dumping the backpack on the table to search through it, but Finn knew there was no time, and anyway, she wouldn't know what to do with a weapon.

"Argh, there's just books, pictures, what the hell?"

Toby threw the backpack to the floor in disgust, as another explosion erupted, closer this time. Finn pulled out one of the chairs which had been pushed into the table, and crawled under the table itself. Toby took one last glance at the doors and windows, and did the same.

"I guess we just hope that it's our guys winning, right? We don't look like a threat, do we?"

"It depends who comes through that door," replied Finn, shifting her head so she could see it through the chair legs.

The noise grew louder still – there was shouting now, and screaming. Finn thought she could hear them on the stairs, coming up towards them. Then suddenly, there was silence.

"Stay still," Toby said softly.

Finn nodded, and fixed her eyes on the door. Slowly, it began to open, and Toby clutched at Finn's shoulder. Finn wished he would let her go but was too nervous to say anything. As the figure stepped into the room, Finn gave a sharp yell of surprise and relief. She scrambled out from under the table.

"Oh, I'm so glad to see you again!" said Braithe. She walked so fast over to meet Finn that she almost broke into a run. She hugged her tight, and then let her go, holding her shoulders and looking after carefully at her.

"I can't believe it's only been a few days," Braithe said. Finn could see tears in her eyes. "And Toby. Oh, it's so good to see you again. Look at you. A young man."

Finn looked down at Toby, still getting up from the floor, and noticed he was blushing.

She hesitated for a moment before continuing, speaking more quickly than before.

"I've got some bad news, though. We've got through to Seven Rivers," Braithe continued. "There was... a conflict."

Finn looked at her, blankly.

"What conflict?" Toby asked.

"It seems that Eva sent transports to Seven Rivers to collect people. Round them up, maybe? Some of the residents resisted – well, I expect they all did, to be fair. And there were some injuries. Casualties."

She paused.

"Jhara is OK. Serena has been badly hurt. There was at least one death."

"Do we know who?" Toby's voice was unsteady. He looked ill.

"Judith."

This time Braithe didn't bother to wipe away the tears. Finn tried to picture the energetic woman, suddenly lifeless. She felt a lump in her throat that made it hard to swallow.

"It doesn't make any sense," Toby said. "Before she...

jumped, Eva seemed convinced the Resistance would win. She seemed… it was as if she was just giving up."

"Maybe she was," said Braithe, "but the rest of them aren't. Thankfully we have several Rescuers on our side, or we'd have no chance. Knowing Eva, she just didn't want to see the fight. She's always been that way. She wants to have the last word. If she can't have something, she… destroys it."

Braithe sighed, and rubbed the back of her neck. It seemed that she wasn't sharing everything she knew, but Finn was too tired to find out. Outside it was still quiet, and Finn felt tempted to go over to the window to see what was happening, but remembered Eva might still be there.

"So what now?" he asked. "I was expecting some huge battle, and now… it's over?"

Braithe pulled out a chair and sat down heavily.

"The City will fall to us tonight, no doubt about that. The rest of the Rescuers will give up. They're security personnel, not soldiers."

She spread her palms out across the table and Finn was reminded of Jhara.

"And everyone at Seven Rivers?" Finn asked. "Bright

Falls?"

"We're still in touch. As soon as everything is secure here, we'll send transports there, collect the wounded, bring them back to the City for treatment."

She paused and looked at Finn.

"The World is still offline. That means we can't reach any of our groups in other cities."

"She knew," whispered Finn.

"Who?" asked Toby.

"Eva. She knew what we were planning to do." Finn turned to Toby. "Remember what she said? She said she'd been watching us. She knew if everyone found out about Western City falling, they'd realise it had begun. And now we can't tell them."

"They'll suspect something, though. With the whole World being down," Toby suggested.

"Maybe?" Finn shrugged. "It could be only local. That happens for maintenance, periodically. I won't know until I get into WorldSec and find out. I don't even know if I'll be able to..."

"Well, we'll have to try," Braithe said. "If we don't get it back up soon, it won't be just the Resistance who are wondering what has happened to us. PlanetRescue might send scouts from other sectors. We won't be able to face them with the numbers we have. Without the World, we've lost."

"No pressure," murmured Toby to Finn, and she flashed a smile.

Braithe stood up.

"There's a Rescuer on guard at the bottom of the stairs. Even if it's quietening down, I want you to let him take you both to WorldSec. You'll be safe there – it was cleared out before you even arrived."

Toby began gathering up the books and pictures. He still looked as if he wanted to ask more questions, but Braithe had already begun to stride back over to the door, and seemed impatient to get going. She had a new energy to her that Finn hadn't seen before. She wondered how much of Braithe had been hidden all these years in the City as they planned for this moment. Finn thought she might even be enjoying it.

They followed Braithe down the stairs, Toby still silent. As they reached the door, she stopped.

"He was here..." Braithe murmured. "He was supposed

to wait here."

She turned to look at them, puzzled, and if Finn were reading her expression correctly, frightened. The confidence she had shown upstairs seemed to have vanished.

Finn wished she knew what to say, but any words disappeared as she saw a dark figure – a Rescuer – walk around the doorway and step quietly behind Braithe. Finn glanced over at Toby, who looked as horrified as she felt. The Rescuer had a tear in his uniform at his left shoulder.

"Braithe!" Finn managed to gasp, and Braithe turned to come face to face with the Rescuer.

"Lowan!" she said, her voice high with obvious relief. "I was worried something had happened to you. As you can see, they're fine."

She smiled and turned to point at Finn and Toby. Lowan pulled off his balaclava and nodded at them both.

"I don't know if you recognise Lowan. He was the one who..."

"The one who threatened us with a stunner at Bright Falls," finished Toby.

"I couldn't break cover," Lowan said. He shrugged and did seem a bit apologetic, Finn thought.

"We knew Eva was aware that we'd infiltrated the Rescuers," Braithe explained, "but we weren't sure how much she knew. So there wasn't any chance for Lowan to let his guard down. But you can trust him. I guarantee it."

Lowan put his hand out to press palms with Finn and then Toby.

"Let's head to WorldSec then?" he said. "I'll take you round the back of the council block. We shouldn't have any problems, but better to be cautious."

He shook his stunner to arm it, and stepped back outside, looking both ways and then gesturing for Finn and Toby to follow.

"Go on," Braithe urged. "I have to get back. There's a lot going on."

"Be safe," Finn managed to blurt out, and Braithe smiled and placed her hand briefly on Finn's cheek.

"I will. This will soon be over. It has been a busy time for you, hasn't it? But we're nearly there."

She, too, looked both ways as she crossed the threshold and then walked quickly across the road to the next block, near the front gate where Finn and Toby had entered.

"Come on," said Lowan. He seemed impatient.

Lowan walked fast and Finn had to run to keep up. By the time they were at the corner opposite the WorldSec block, she resented him for her aching ankles and shortness of breath. It was quiet in this area. Once her breathing slowly returned to normal, Finn could hear the odd shout and crash in the distance, but around WorldSec there was nobody else. She felt suddenly very vulnerable. Toby seemed to sense her fear.

"I have a good feeling about him," he said. "We'll be fine. Let's get inside and you can see what's up with the World."

Lowan, already over the road and checking down the side of the WorldSec block, waved to get their attention.

WorldSec was usually an efficiently run area, with just the right number of personnel at any time. Finn breathed in. The blandness of the air was a relief compared to the constantly moving sensory assault of the Badlands. She had missed this.

Finn put her hands on the nearest desk. It was cool and smooth, familiar. She had never been in WorldSec at night, but it was simple to imagine that it was a normal day, that her colleagues were sitting as they usually were, logged in via the link, eyes closed, hands flat on desks as they worked, barely making a sound. The quiet was one of her favourite aspects of her work. That, and the challenge. The discovery of holes in the Ether needing repair, the back doors, and then the parts of the World only accessible to those with top clearance, like herself.

It had been so many hours since she had had quiet thinking time. Time to reorder and sort the experiences of the past hours and days – the revelation of her parents, the history and stories of everyone in Seven Rivers. She thought of Judith with all her energy, now lying silent and still somewhere; of Eva, disappearing over the edge of the building. Finn shuddered. It was too difficult and confusing. Better to focus on what she had to do now. Focus on the future, not on the dead and the past.

Finn reached the panel at the far wall and slid her fingers down the smooth edge until she felt a click of the catch. She opened the panel to reveal rows of cabling – the central hub. Finn relaxed at the sight of it. Neat and logical, exactly what she had missed. She reached over to the row of switches at the side and was about to flick the first one across to reset, when there was a crash from behind. Finn whipped around to Lowan and Toby struggling against two other Rescuers in the doorway to WorldSec, a confusion of arms and legs and grunts as the four of them fought over the threshold.

She rushed forward, running towards them, even as she realised she wasn't at all sure what to do. As she reached the others, she slowed, then pushed off suddenly with her left foot, slamming her shoulder into the Rescuer who was fighting Toby. It caught him off guard, and his stunner slipped out of his grasp and onto the ground. Finn quickly dug her elbow into his stomach and stomped on his foot. The element of surprise had worked beautifully.

Toby fell to the ground as well, just down the steps of WorldSec, and he scrabbled towards the stunner, even as the Rescuer recovered and stretched across to get it back. Finn squeezed her fists tight, and held them under her chin, holding her breath as all four of them continued to fight. Now the other Rescuers knew she was there, she wasn't sure how else to disrupt it all, and she closed her eyes and began to shuffle backwards, wanting the violence to end, but powerless to stop it.

She heard a stunner discharge, twice, then once more. Three stabs of charge, four people. She began to feel dizzy and gasped for breath.

"Finn," said a voice, then more insistent, "Finn. Open your eyes."

Toby stood in front of her.

"You missed my big moment. Well, mine and Lowan's. Hey, Lowan?"

They both looked at Lowan lying face down on the ground, hands flat against the smooth surface, as if he were about to push his body upright to join them. He moaned faintly. Finn and Toby looked at each other.

"What do we do?" asked Finn. She couldn't decide if she should touch him or not.

"We need help," Toby said. "How do I get to Braithe?"

Finn dragged her gaze from Lowan, and looked to Toby.

"You go..." She shook her head trying to clear it. "You go back the way we came, past the next two blocks..."

She described the building where Braithe would be.

"You'll be OK?" Toby said.

Finn nodded.

"I need to work on getting the World back up."

"I'll be as fast as I can," said Toby, and set off at a jog.

Finn nodded, turned, walking slowly back into the room. Maybe it would all be easier to accept, if she could just return to the World, slip into the Ether, fix the obvious mistakes, instead of having to deal with all this. These betrayals and violence, this sudden end of life from one moment to the next.

She reached the mainframe, once again taking comfort in it. Resetting it was simple, just a matter of knowing the right switches, the correct combinations. It was all about putting everything back where it should be.

Finn replaced the cover, clicking it into place. In the silence, the sound was satisfying. As she switched in her mind, she saw the clumsy mistakes her colleagues had made as they were attempting to shut down the World forever. They'd been following orders – she doubted they understood what they had been tasked with. The World spread out before her. She felt others connecting, those she knew well, those she didn't. She contacted Braithe.

I'm in. I'm fixing it, all of it. We can do this.

I knew you could do it, Braithe replied.

But it was so simple.

For you, maybe. There was a smile behind her thoughts.

But going to the Badlands, to Seven Rivers? I could have stayed here and done this. I could have…

You needed to see, Finn, Braithe interrupted her, *where you'd come from, what was at stake. You needed to feel like you were part of this whole thing. And they needed that from you, too. Do you understand?*

Finn was quiet. Did she understand? There had been so much input over the past days. New people, re-connections to a past she had forgotten. She thought it might take months to process it all.

I understand.

I have to gather people together. It's better if I tell them in person, what's next for us. Come to our block.

Finn closed her eyes and paused a moment.

Toby should be there in a minute. Lowan is hurt and needs help. Finn realised that etiquette dictated that she should have probably mentioned Lowan's injury first.

I'll send people to meet him, Braithe reassured her. *Are you coming?*

I want to stay here where it's quiet, for a bit. Finish repairs.

Do that. I'll contact you when the transports come in from Seven Rivers.

Finn let go of the link. She walked over to the side door

and opened it up, standing on the small balcony. She looked out towards the east, the direction in which she and Jhara had left days before. Through the dome, Finn thought she could see the brightening of the sky. It seemed so dull, hardly half the light and colour of the brilliance she knew was there, outside in the Badlands. Barely even real, filtered as it was through the membrane. But she knew it was there. Smiling, she stretched her arms out wide, towards the edge of the dome, towards the hills to the east and the ocean to the west. The distance seemed to push back and pull forwards and stretch all around her.

It was good to be home.

REBECCA FREEMAN

About the Author

Rebecca Freeman is a freelance editor and writer. She lives on the south coast of Western Australia with her Handsome Sidekick and their too many children and pets. You can find her online:

Website: https://www.rebeccafreeman.com.au/
Facebook: https://www.facebook.com/bec.lloyd.freeman
Instagram: https://www.instagram.com/words_by_rebecca/

www.ingramcontent.com/pod-product-compliance
Lightning Source LLC
Chambersburg PA
CBHW071357100726
47908CB00004B/1029